UPSTART

LOW BLOW #4

CHARITY PARKERSON

--Warning: This book is intended for readers over the age of 18.

Copyright © 2017 Charity Parkerson
Editor: Hercules and Consultants
Photographer: Taria Reed|The Reed Files

ISBN: 978-1-946099-19-8

❀ Created with Vellum

INTRODUCTION

Two men with no interest in being tied down. Each incapable of staying away from the other. Who will be the first to break?

For years, Daniel has traveled the world, enjoying the benefits of his position with the *Daily Sports Report.* He's always loved all things sports. This is his passion. He's never met a man who can tempt him to slow down. No promises of love can match the dream he's already living, until Isaac.

Isaac isn't starving for anything. He's closer to achieving his dreams than ever, thanks to the world's best trainer taking him in. Men throw themselves his way, keeping him fed sexually. Isaac doesn't need a relationship holding him back. That is, until a sexy sports journalist invites Isaac back to his hotel room.

No matter how hard the men try avoiding each other, they can't seem to stop crossing paths. An attraction becomes a connection. A connection becomes an obsession. If they're not careful, an obsession will become a love worth losing everything for.

1

Upstart: A new fighter with potential.

*A*ugust

A thousand tiny life decisions had led Isaac here, putting him in the position where he currently sat—across from one of the most well-known sports reporters, being given a lesson on guarding his private life from the press. Possibly, he was here because one of MMA's greatest fighters, Drew Alexander, believed in him enough to send Isaac here. Not everyone training with Drew got the chance to take part in Aden Dawley's program. Maybe he was here because he'd worked for it. After all, Aden was considered the all-time best boxing trainer in the world. Isaac just wanted to fight. He didn't care who taught him. If Drew had sent him to the ends of the Earth, Isaac would've gone for the chance to win. The truth of how he'd landed here was dumb luck.

Daniel Long had one of those names. Isaac saw it everywhere and dreamed the man would one day write about him. He'd never thought about the man behind the name.

Isaac's thoughts had centered more on his own fame. Now, Isaac had to reassess those fantasies, adding the image of Daniel to each. The dude was hot. Granted, it was a hipster kind of hot, and that had never really been Isaac's thing, but damn. Staring at Daniel's full lips and sexy light-brown eyes had Isaac digging a night of poetry readings or whatever hipsters did with their time.

"Are you dating anyone?" Daniel's question dragged Isaac from his fantasy of what those lips could do.

"Are you asking for yourself or for a friend?"

Daniel's mouth lifted in one corner, making his smile the wickedest Isaac had ever seen. "I'm testing you. Which questions do you answer? How much do you care if the public knows? What's off limits? So, are you seeing anyone?"

"I see people all day," Isaac said, biting back a smile.

"Well, I imagine training keeps you busy," Daniel countered, as if Isaac's dodging was all the answer he needed. "Plus, since you're not a household name... yet," Daniel said, adding the perfect pause for flattery. "I'm sure you also work to pay bills."

"Yes."

Daniel nodded and dropped his gaze to his phone as if Isaac's banter was beginning to bore him.

Isaac couldn't stop staring at the man's mouth. He wanted the wicked smile back. "I'm a doorman for one of Las Vegas's most exclusive fetish clubs."

Daniel's gaze slowly lifted from his phone. His eyes danced with laughter. "That's definitely one of the things you'll want to keep private during a real interview."

Isaac caught himself leaning closer. "Does that mean everything said here is off the record?"

"Of course," Daniel said, falling back into a placid demeanor. "This meeting is for educational purposes. Aden never would've recruited me for this if he thought I'd print these sessions."

"I didn't doubt your professionalism. Just clarifying the details."

Daniel put his phone away and gave Isaac his undivided attention. "Since we've established I'll keep your secrets, tell me everything."

"That would take all night," Isaac said, incapable of not flirting for some reason.

"It's eleven in the morning."

Neither of them looked away from the other. "I'm aware," Isaac said, unconcerned.

"We should go back to my hotel room."

Daniel's bored-sounding tone never wavered, but Isaac didn't misunderstand. For a moment, he was rendered speechless. He cleared his throat. "Um. Is this part of your test?"

The wicked smile was back. "No. This is a special onetime invitation."

Isaac wouldn't make the man ask him twice. "We should get the check."

At his response, Daniel cast a glance around the restaurant. Obviously spotting the waitress somewhere behind Isaac, Daniel motioned the woman closer before pulling two twenties from his pocket, throwing them on the table, and coming to his feet. "Are you ready?"

Isaac was used to being the one who paid, but—at the moment—he had bigger things on his mind. "Absolutely." They were inside Daniel's rental and halfway to the hotel before Isaac found his voice again. "I see you everywhere. Where do you actually live?"

Daniel kept his gaze locked on the road as he answered. "Out of a suitcase, mostly. I also have an apartment in New

York." He flashed a smile Isaac's way. "I haven't seen it in six months."

"It must be amazing, getting to travel and see the world." Isaac was merely filling the silence with noise. He needed the distraction. When he'd told Daniel where he worked, he'd done so for many reasons. The most obvious one was to shock the man. It had also been a warning. Isaac was a sexual person. In truth, he was what most people would consider a kink. He might work the door at Affinity, but Isaac was also a member. There wasn't much Isaac hadn't tried. As long as everyone was legal and consenting, he was in. Sometimes, he could be too intense.

"It is," Daniel said, pulling Isaac's thoughts back on topic. "But I don't think you care. I think you're making conversation for the sake of conversation."

Daniel had him there. "Saying I don't care might be taking it a bit far, but—since you're driving—I didn't think you'd want me doing this," Isaac said, running his hand up Daniel's thigh.

Daniel covered Isaac's hand with his and held it in place. "I think you're closer to being in your element now instead of making awkward small talk."

"Maybe I just want to watch the way your sexy lips move."

The naughty smile Isaac craved was back in place. He couldn't look away. "I get the feeling you're so much better when you're bad."

Isaac skimmed Daniel's cock with the side of his hand. "I guess we'll find out."

A dimple appeared in Daniel's cheek, but he didn't respond. The hotel came into sight. Isaac took a deep breath and put his work face on. He was rarely real with anyone. A one-night stand was the perfect example. They rode the elevator up in silence. That didn't stop Isaac from staring at Daniel. He let the heat between them rise. Daniel's gaze slid his way. It didn't budge. Isaac's lips curled into a knowing smile. This man—he would be amazing. Daniel wasn't shy or wilting. He wanted what he wanted and didn't hide it. Hunger tightened Isaac's groin.

While Daniel swiped his keycard, Isaac eyed Daniel's body. The man wasn't tall. He was perhaps only an inch shorter than Isaac. At five-eleven, it wasn't unusual for Isaac to date taller men. Although Daniel was basically the same height as Isaac, he wasn't as large. Instead, he had the tight body of a runner with sleek muscles and an ass only squats could achieve. It took all of Isaac's willpower not to mold his body against Daniel's as he crossed the threshold of his room. Instead, Isaac chose to stalk him. His gaze ate the man alive as he closed the door behind him. It was obvious Daniel made way more money than Isaac. Isaac had a basic room, paid for by Drew. Daniel had a suite with a huge bed and full kitchen—not that Isaac bothered checking out the place. His focus was held captive by the way Daniel moved. Isaac let his hunger grow.

"This is a nice room."

"It is," Daniel said, pulling out a chair from the table. He sat. His gaze followed Isaac's every move. "Take your clothes off."

It seemed Daniel didn't mess around. That was fine. Isaac was tired of pretending his dick didn't throb with anticipation. He tugged his shirt up and over his head without argument. As he slid his workout pants down his hips, Daniel's gaze hooded and he relaxed deeper in his seat. He swiped his hand over his erection, drawing Isaac's gaze to the way it strained against the man's expensive dress pants. Isaac's cock sprang free, and he shoved his pants the rest of the way down. He'd been training and fighting for the MMA circuit for years. Isaac knew how he looked. He spent more hours at the gym every day than most people slept. His body was a weapon. Right now, he wanted to use it against the sexy journalist who sat watching his every move.

The instant he was completely bare, Daniel motioned him closer. "Come here." Daniel's chin tilted up as Isaac came to stand over him. The man's gorgeous eyes flashed with so much desire, it weakened Isaac's knees. "I wonder what your deepest, darkest fantasies are?"

"Fantasies are for people who are starved of what they really want. I'm well fed." Even to his ears, Isaac sounded aroused. The erection tapping his navel was the second clue.

Daniel's gaze swept Isaac's body. Heat singed each place his stare touched. He took off his glasses and set them aside. The man's light- brown eyes were even more gorgeous when the light hit them. Daniel sat forward. "You might be well fed, but I'm starved." Without warning, Daniel fisted Isaac's cock and took him to the back of his throat.

Isaac's fingers were in the man's hair, holding on for dear life before he knew what happened. His knees were weak. All he could do was watch and feel. Daniel didn't hold back. Isaac wasn't small by any stretch of the imagination and Daniel swallowed him with ease. Isaac fought to breathe. His balls were already tight. Daniel massaged them before urging Isaac's thighs apart. Isaac complied. Daniel toyed with his asshole, teasing him. Isaac stared down his body, battling against his heavy eyelids. They wanted to fall closed and savor the sensations. Isaac needed to watch.

An odd thought sneaked in as Daniel curled one finger inside him. They hadn't kissed. Isaac saw most of his action inside Affinity. He'd been blindfolded and sucked off by people whose faces he'd never even seen. Yet, this was still the most impersonal blow job he'd ever had. Not that he wasn't enjoying it. The hot pull of Daniel's mouth had Isaac's nerve endings dancing. He gasped for air. His hips moved, pumping against Daniel's sexy lips. He scraped against the roof of the man's mouth and easily slid down his throat—over and over again at the perfect pace. His muscles tensed. He squeezed his ass cheeks together, clenching around Daniel's fingers. His hold tightened on the man's hair. Daniel sucked hard. The universe held its breath. Everything went silent. An explosion of ecstasy hit Isaac, rocking him on his feet. He cried out as wave after wave filled Daniel's mouth with cum. The man didn't slow. He sucked, drinking Isaac down and pulling more from Isaac than he'd ever given. His muscles twitched.

Daniel shot to his feet. His mouth covered Isaac's. The flavor of his orgasm still coated Daniel's tongue. Isaac tried sucking it away. Daniel's kiss was rougher than Isaac imagined. He was raw and in control. It was as if Daniel had read Isaac's user manual and knew all his kinks. Isaac liked being manhandled. Loved it, actually. In his real life, Isaac was always in charge. When he hit the sheets, he wanted something else. The way Daniel kept biting him said he knew. Isaac worked the buttons loose on the man's shirt before pushing it down his arms.

Daniel backed away. He looked hard and unreachable. His focused gaze and swollen lips had Isaac ready to beg. Daniel tossed his shirt to the floor. His hands went for his belt. "Face down on the bed."

At Daniel's rough tone, Isaac bit back a whimper. He'd claimed he didn't have any fantasies. Daniel was proving him wrong. Without argument, he did as told. He moved to the bed and immediately went face down and ass up. Isaac could hear Daniel moving around behind him. The familiar sound of a condom wrapper crinkling filled the air. Cool liquid swiped his asshole. Isaac's dick twitched like it hadn't just been sucked dry. Daniel massaged the globes of his ass, spreading his cheeks wide as he moved in behind him. Isaac bit his bottom lip and held his breath. He couldn't remember the last time he'd been this horny. For years, he'd suffered from little more than a passing interest in anyone. He enjoyed himself, but that was about it. Daniel had him panting. On the verge of begging.

"Tell me again how you have no fantasies," Daniel taunted as he stretched Isaac's asshole. The whimper he'd been biting back escaped. "I disagree," Daniel added, sounding hard. "In fact, I think you've been dying inside while waiting for someone like me to recognize you should be on your knees. Now beg me to fuck you." Daniel twisted his fingers and pushed on the knot inside Isaac that would make him do anything for more.

"Please, Daniel." He couldn't stop panting. "I need it."

A low, condescending chuckle filled the air behind him. "Need what?"

"Your dick inside me," Isaac said without hesitation. "I need you to fuck me hard." As the words fell, Daniel impaled him, giving Isaac the rough treatment he craved. Isaac's ears rang. Nothing penetrated the noise but the sound of skin slapping skin. Isaac scratched at the sheets and his dick leaked on the bed. He fisted his begging cock, tugging and pulling—blind with lust. He craved. Ached. Most of all, Isaac saw stars. If he breathed, he couldn't remember it. All of his focus locked on Daniel fucking him into oblivion. The man was huge. Isaac's asshole burned from the abuse. He craved more—loved the pain. Another orgasm tore through him. A roar of pleasure ripped from his throat. His ass clamped down on Daniel's dick, trying to pull him deeper.

Daniel's moans filled the room. Satisfaction owned Isaac. He was the reason Daniel made those sounds. They collapsed into a heap of sweat and cum, their bodies sticking together. Daniel's hot breath fanned out across the back of Isaac's neck.

"Fucking amazing."

Pride like Isaac had never felt roared through him, rocking him to his core. He'd won fights and achieved every goal he set. Nothing he'd done in his life gave him the satisfaction Daniel's praise caused. The knowledge fucked with his head. He shouldn't care. He wouldn't care. This had been a onetime thing.

2

*J*une

For three months, Isaac had been sitting on a secret. After tonight, everyone would know. If he won, he would smile and say his goals had changed when he hadn't been looking. If he lost, he'd have no other choice than to hang his head in shame and pray Drew Alexander didn't boot him from his MMA training program.

The crowd inside Lummaxx arena was huge. It was the biggest crowd he'd fought in front of before. As the officials signed off on his gloves, Isaac tried not to bounce on his toes. His nerves were on edge. He couldn't let them get the best of him. Things had changed for him before he knew what happened. One night, he'd been down in Key Largo, training with an ex-boxing-champ, Remy Dawley. Even though he fought the MMA circuit, he'd come to realize the ex-champ had a lot to offer. Remy had jokingly bet Isaac he couldn't beat a boxer. That was where it started. They'd driven into Miami, found an open Friday night fight, and Isaac had signed up. To everyone's surprise, he'd won. It hadn't been a pretty win. It had been hard not to use his feet or holds. When it was over, Isaac had been pumped. He'd beat a man using nothing more than his fists and wits. Two weeks later, he'd searched Vegas for a match. He'd entered and won again. The obsession grew. He loved MMA. Isaac was good at it, but boxing... he was better. A month later, with a few more wins under his belt, Isaac had secretly changed his training around and gotten serious about taking down bigger targets. That was how he ended up here —in front of a screaming crowd and taking on an opponent who'd been on track for a belt for much longer than Isaac.

Isaac dipped between the ropes and hoped he wouldn't puke. His cornerman—an old friend from school, Marcus— stood at Isaac's back. The rules were read. Isaac rolled his shoulders. The noise around him turned into a buzz before completely disappearing. Laser focus settled in. He could smell the old sweat and leather. Everything became clear— like he held up a magnifying glass to his opponent. The man was taller, but it was all legs. Isaac had the reach. Gregor McCully—the man bouncing on his toes and giving Isaac the evil eye — knew he would win. Isaac was easy pickings, except Isaac wasn't. He wanted this too badly. The thought of facing Drew about giving up his MMA dream with a loss weighing on his shoulders was too much. He had to beat this big fucker.

The bell rang. They danced. Gregor jabbed first. Isaac dodged. So, it began. The first four rounds were nothing. They both took hits and gave them. Neither of them showed any signs of slowing. Isaac had stamina. He could last. The bell rang again. Time slowed. Isaac's vision narrowed to a pinpoint. He could hear his heart pounding in his ears. Gregor shifted unexpectedly, dropping his hands, obviously intent on a left swing. Instead, Isaac stole his chance, striking quick. His hit his mark. He watched as the world slowed to a crawl. Gregor rocked on his heels, dropping his gloves. Isaac struck again, landing a solid right hook across the side of the man's head before following it with a left. Gregor went down. The referee pushed him out of the way. Isaac hovered at the edge, holding his breath and watching the count. Gregor tried rolling to his knees. The count continued. Another bell ring declared Isaac the winner. His shock was complete. He'd done it. Isaac hadn't failed. He had his new start.

Isaac didn't even make it to his SUV before his cell-phone rang. He glanced at the face, spotting Drew's number. He almost didn't answer. In the end, he decided a phone call beat a face-to-face any day of the week.

"Hello?"

"I'm guessing this means you hope I'll take on training another boxer."

By Drew's tone, Isaac already knew that hope was futile. "I know things didn't really work out with Remy, but—to be fair—his place was always with Aden."

"It's more than that," Drew said, sounding tired. "The Remy experiment proved cross training doesn't work at No Rival. That's the whole reason I've got all of you on rotation, sending you down Aden's way. As much as none of you want to accept it, I'm tired. I want to spend time with my kids. It's getting to be about time for me to pass the reins on to someone else."

Isaac tossed his gym bag in the back seat of his Tahoe and climbed behind the wheel. He chewed his bottom lip, trying to decide what to do. He'd always known convincing Drew to train him was a long shot. After all, Drew trained champs. Isaac didn't have much hope of ever obtaining that level.

"I'm sorry, Isaac," Drew said, sounding genuinely apologetic. "From what I've heard, you've got a real shot at this, but I can't be your man."

Isaac scrubbed his hand over his face. "It's okay, Drew. I know you can't be all things to all people."

"Best of luck to you."

Isaac nodded, even though Drew couldn't see, and while wondering why it felt a lot like he'd been dumped. "Thanks. Talk to you later."

"Yep. Congrats. You'll work it out."

He would. Isaac always landed on his feet.

ADEN'S HOUSE WAS GORGEOUS. The large home was set high. Isaac assumed it was that way to avoid high tide or storms. He eyed the red Dodge and black F150 in the drive. It seemed both men were home. Still, he rang the doorbell, debating on whether he wanted it answered. He'd made the trip, putting a huge dent in his savings. It was ridiculous to let nerves get the best of him now. Isaac needed this.

The door swung wide. The red-haired giant stared out at him. For a moment, Isaac found himself speechless. Aden was shirtless, wearing nothing more than flowered swim trunks. He'd always known the man's clothes covered some massive muscles. Isaac still hadn't been prepared. Aden looked like he could snap a man in two.

He scratched at his scraggly jaw as if trying to figure out why Isaac was there. "Isaac. You're a long way from home."

Isaac nodded. It wasn't as if he could claim he'd simply been in the neighborhood. "I've been needing a vacation, so I decided to kill two birds with one stone and stop by."

Even though Aden looked like Isaac's explanation was about as clear as mud, he still took a step back. "Come on in," Aden said as he turned, leading Isaac through the house. "Gunnar opened the gym today. If you're here to ask permission to train while you're in town, I'm cool with that, but I'd have to call and let Gunnar know."

Isaac shut the door behind him and followed on Aden's heels. "Thanks. That's good to know. Actually, I hoped to talk to you about something else."

"I hope you brought your trunks, because Remy is dead set on no work and all play today."

This was about work. Isaac almost turned around right then. If he knew nothing else, he knew making Remy unhappy would guarantee Aden turned him down. "This will only take a second."

Aden led Isaac to a small oak kitchen table. After taking a seat, he motioned for Isaac to sit as well. As Isaac did as bade, his gaze locked on the gorgeous emerald-colored water shimmering from the gulf through the French doors at Aden's back. It was as if they were sitting directly on the water. "It's beautiful here."

"It is," Remy said, appearing at Isaac's back and startling him. He moved around Isaac to Aden's side. Isaac's gaze dropped to Remy's ass as he passed. It was out of his control. He wasn't attracted to Remy in that way. Not that Remy wasn't incredibly sexy. He simply wasn't Isaac's type. The ass-ogling was for another reason. Remy wore a bright red speedo with the words "This ass won't spank itself" printed across the back. Remy stopped next to Aden and poked his ass out, leaving Aden no other choice but to inspect it. The luminous smile touching Aden's lips and swimming in his eyes had Isaac grinning like a fool. It was impossible to be in the presence of so much happiness and not be affected.

"You'll have to wait until our guest leaves," Aden said, his Irish accent thickening.

"I'm patient," Remy said, snagging a barstool from the island that separated the dining room from the kitchen. "Hiya, Isaac. How's it going?" Remy asked as he plopped down on the stool.

"Things are going good, thanks," Isaac said, trying to fight his laughter.

It seemed the barstool spun—much to Remy's delight. He turned in a circle while he spoke, repeating Aden's earlier comment. "I hope you came to swim, because we're on staycation."

"Honestly, I only need like five minutes of your time."

"We have trunks you could borrow," Remy said, staring at the ceiling while spinning his chair.

Isaac waved off his offer. "Actually, mine are in my luggage in the car. I'm on vacation too, but I'm just here to ask a favor."

"You could ask your favor while wearing swimming trunks and soaking up some vitamin D."

Isaac's cheeks ached at Remy's stubbornness. It should've driven him nuts, but it was impossible to be irritated with someone like Remy. He was like an over-caffeinated puppy in designer clothes.

"I've decided to switch from the MMA circuit to boxing." Remy stopped spinning at Isaac's announcement. "Actually, ever since I won that fight in Miami, I've won several more."

Remy brightened. "Ha. I brought you to the good side."

"That's not possible," Isaac said with a wink before he could stop himself. He quickly reeled himself in before Aden thought he was flirting. "But I do need help."

"No," Aden said, coming to his feet, and bringing their discussion to an end before it began.

"You didn't hear me out."

Aden focused on him. His face softened. "Look, it's not

personal. You live in Vegas and I've already turned down Drew's offer to work for No Rival. My heart is here," Aden said, motioning toward Remy. "I won't take away from him to give to anyone else."

"What if I moved here?" Isaac asked without thought.

Aden didn't answer right away. It gave him hope. When he finally spoke, Isaac felt hope slipping away. "Can you afford to do that? You do realize I'm expensive. Not to mention, the big fights are everywhere but here. Can you afford the constant travel? If not, you'd be better off staying at No Rival and letting Drew train you. At least there, you'd have access to pot fights."

With every word Aden spoke, Isaac's heart sank. It wasn't that he hadn't considered those things. He just hadn't wanted to look at things too closely. Isaac had thought if Aden was willing, then he'd find a way. It didn't seem Aden was willing. He thought he might hyperventilate. Remy was back to spinning and staring at the ceiling. Isaac hadn't wanted anything like he craved this, and he couldn't see his way toward achieving it.

"He could work for us at the training center and stay in the empty apartment above the place. That way, he could save his money for travel," Remy suggested, proving he was listening despite his playing around.

Hope reignited. His gaze locked on Aden, searching for any chance the man might cave. Aden looked thoughtful.

Remy stopped spinning and focused on his husband. "It would be extra work for you to train another fighter, but then again, it wouldn't, because I'd help, and having him as an extra on-site employee would give you more time with me."

Aden ignored Isaac's presence while he stared at his husband. "I'll do whatever you decide."

Remy nodded. He focused on Isaac and smiled. "Grab your trunks and join us for the day. Let's see if you can handle the mess that we are for longer than an hour at a time."

So much had taken place in Remy and Aden's conversation that would change Isaac's life forever, he didn't know what to say. What had started as an impulsive offer to move had transformed into a new job and a place to live in under five minutes. Isaac couldn't stop smiling, but he feared he looked every bit as shell-shocked as he felt. "Sure thing. I'd love to spend the day with you." Isaac meant it. He just hoped he didn't pass out from living a life turned on its head.

*a*den's training facility smelled like all the things Daniel loved—sports, leather, and sweaty men. He'd intentionally arrived fifteen minutes earlier so he could check in with his boss before the new batch of No Rival trainees arrived. Since Aden stood a foot taller than everyone else, Daniel spotted the red-haired giant right away. Aden dipped his chin, acknowledging Daniel's arrival.

"It's good to see you, Daniel."

"You as well," Daniel said with a genuine smile. Despite Aden's constant growls and grumbles, Daniel liked the abrasive man. Anyone who had what it took to win Remy couldn't be all that bad. "Do you care if I use your office to make a quick call before we get started? I have to let my boss know where I am."

Aden waved him away. "Aye. Knock yourself out."

Daniel didn't need to be told twice. He pulled his cellphone from his back pocket as he cleared the door. His boss, Phil, had the most annoying voicemail in history. It picked up on the fourth ring. Daniel hung up before he had to sit through it. He needed to check in, but a text would have to do if the man wouldn't answer his phone.

"Probably out playing golf," Daniel muttered under his breath as he shot off a quick message.

"Dear god. It looks like a rainbow threw up in here."

Daniel spun at the claim. His body hummed at the first sight of Isaac. It had been ten months. Not that he'd been counting. After taking a breath to hide his excitement, Daniel turned in a slow circle, inspecting the chalk rainbow-colored drawings on the walls to buy himself another second before responding. "It looks like the inside of Remy's unicorn brain. I love it. He makes the world a better place. Not many people do." Daniel wanted to pat himself on the back for pulling off a bored tone.

Isaac's amber-colored gaze swept Daniel's body. Daniel had a hard time pretending the man's gorgeous chocolate-colored skin and sleek muscles didn't faze him. "Does Aden know you have a thing for Remy?"

Isaac didn't sound jealous, merely curious. It made Daniel want to rattle him. "Yes. Why do you think he always introduces me to everyone as 'the little bastard'? What brings you around?" Daniel asked without giving Isaac time to answer his first question. "I knew the new batch of hope-fuls from No Rival were coming today, but since you've already been through Drew's life lessons course, I'm confused as to why you're back."

"I forgot about your interview training," Isaac said, as if the words had been meant for himself. They still stung. Damn. Apparently, he'd been forgettable. Isaac cleared his throat as he moved to sit behind Aden's desk. "I work here now. This is my first day," he added, flashing Daniel a smile.

He hadn't been expecting that tidbit. "You work here? Seriously? Why?"

Isaac barely spared him a glance as he dug through the drawers of Aden's desk. "Is this on the record?"

"Everything is always on the record with me," Daniel shot back.

Isaac froze and met Daniel's gaze. "Fine. I moved down here so Aden could train me. You never called."

For a moment, all Daniel could do was blink at the rapid change of topic. "Does anyone call?"

Isaac's eyebrows damn near hit his hairline at Daniel's question. He hadn't meant to sound cold. Daniel tried clarifying his statement. "I meant, under the circumstances of our last meeting, do most people call?" He wasn't sure if that was better, but fuck. This was uncomfortable. He hadn't thought about what he'd say if they saw each other again, and he'd never been good at personal interaction outside his job.

"I guess not," Isaac said, pulling a set of keys from Aden's desk. He stood and nodded in Daniel's direction. "Good seeing you again, Daniel. I'll get out of your hair."

Damn. He couldn't stop watching that ass walk away. Isaac hadn't sounded hurt or disappointed. More like he was done. Daniel didn't like that. The idea crawled over his skin and fit like a bad suit. He was the one who decided when he was finished with someone. His feet moved without his permission. He needed to get started on his mock interview for the day, but that ass. Daniel was on Isaac's heels like their shoestrings were tied together. He was in town for two more weeks. They should do this. Daniel's mouth watered at the idea. He'd thought about Isaac more than he cared to admit.

"Daniel," Aden barked his name, calling him under control before he took Isaac down like a cheetah on the hunt.

He swung around, recalling where he was. "Yes."

The red-haired giant eyed him. Suspicion dripped from his pores. "You're working with Mateo today."

"Yes," Daniel repeated like a parrot that knew only one word. "Of course." He barely stopped himself from casting one last longing gaze Isaac's way. Instead, he donned his fake persona and focused on the caramel-skinned man waiting for his interview training. "I usually take my dates to lunch. Do you like fish? I hope so," Daniel said, not giving the man a chance to answer. "They don't serve anything else in this million-boat town."

"Fish is good for you," Mateo said, flashing a sexy smile. It did nothing for Daniel.

He sighed. "Another health nut." How tiresome. His smile got harder to fake by the second. "You fit right in around here. I'll drive." Perfect teeth. Perfect hair. Perfectly boring. Daniel already had this one figured out, but he was a favor for Aden. Mateo wasn't part of Drew's program. Instead, he was one of Aden's brightest stars. Everyone expected Mateo would win a title any day now and Daniel would be interviewing him for real soon. Daniel lost the battle against himself and cast a glance Isaac's way. The man's workout pants shaped the curve of his ass to perfection. Daniel could still feel the sexiness beneath his palms.

"Nice, huh?" Mateo said over his shoulder. The man's Brazilian accent thickened. "Aden says he's moving into the apartment above the gym, and he's working here now. That gives me plenty of time to make my move," Mateo added with a wink.

It was a lucky thing Daniel was a master at hiding his reactions. He'd never hated anyone more. "Is that so? Tell me all about it," Daniel said, leading him toward the door. As Daniel had told Isaac, nothing was truly off the record with him. If Mateo moved on Isaac, Daniel would slaughter him in the public eye. He'd lost his moral compass so long ago, he no longer missed it. Isaac submitted to no one except him.

———

"THAT WAS INTERESTING."

"What?" Isaac asked, tearing his gaze away from his feet to focus on Remy. They'd been swapping between unpacking boxes and checking on club business for the past three hours. Of course, for the past five minutes, Isaac had been trying so hard not to look at Daniel, he'd forgotten what they were doing and developed an unhealthy fascination with the toes of his shoes.

"The way Daniel was just staring at you," he said, nodding toward where Daniel held the door open for Mateo, leading the man outside. They had their heads together. Isaac kind of wanted to put his fist through the wall.

Isaac shrugged. "Guess I missed it."

The way Remy stared at him let Isaac know he wasn't fooled. "Okay. It's all right if you don't want to talk to me."

Damned if Remy's hurt tone didn't make him feel like shit. The moment of jealous rage he'd felt at Daniel admitting he wanted Remy had passed as quickly as it began. Daniel was right. Remy was a bright spot in an ugly world. Plus, it was hardly Remy's fault he was always the most beautiful person in the room. There was also the fact that he wouldn't be here at all if Remy hadn't gone to bat for him with Aden. And now, here Remy was following him around and helping him get settled—like a friend would.

He headed for the door. Remy followed him out. Isaac

chewed his bottom lip and debated his next move all the way up the back stairs and into his new apartment before breaking. "So, maybe we slept together."

"Shut. Up." Remy's scandalized tone had Isaac wishing he hadn't been too chicken shit to look at Remy while making the confession. He would've loved to have seen the man's expression.

For some reason, Remy's reaction kept Isaac talking. "It was a onetime thing. If he was looking at me in any way, it was probably him wondering why his past would be biting him in the ass for the next two weeks."

"No, really. Shut. Up," Remy repeated, finally managing to pull Isaac's gaze his way. Isaac wasn't disappointed. The man looked like someone had pantsed him and he was still reeling from the unexpected move.

A laugh escaped Isaac. "Sorry. I'm pretty open—sexually speaking. With me, you might not want to ask anything if you don't really want to know."

Remy motioned wildly. "I don't care about that. If you hang around long enough, it's only a matter of time before you catch Aden and me creeping into his office. That's not it at all. It's Daniel Long. You had sex with Daniel Long?"

Another chuckle escaped Isaac. "Yep."

"Wow," Remy breathed, looking impressed. "Don't get me wrong, I like Daniel a lot. We've spent quite a bit of time with each other over the years, but there's still something about him that intimidates the hell out of me."

Against his will, a bark of loud laughter sneaked past Isaac's lips. "Remy, you're one of the biggest names in boxing. You intimidate people."

Remy shook his head, even as he moved to open another box. "That's not what I mean. I can't explain it. It's in his eyes."

Remy didn't have to explain. Isaac knew. It was in Daniel's eyes. He would never be gentle or loving. Those were qualities someone like Remy needed. Isaac was the opposite. He didn't need someone to pet and hold him. Isaac needed someone to fuck him and make him feel alive.

"None of this matters," Isaac said, ready to let it drop. "It was almost a year ago and only the one time. I don't know what you saw back there."

Remy unearthed a set of plates. "Which cabinet do you want these in?"

"Left of the sink."

As Remy stacked the plates in the cabinet, he kept up his side of the conversation. "You should ask Daniel to join us for Friday night fights in Miami this weekend."

"It's like you didn't hear a word I just said," Isaac said with a laugh.

Remy glanced over his shoulder and winked. "Oh, I heard you, but Daniel can be your best asset or your worst enemy in this business. If he sees your potential for himself, one well-placed article from him could have you leap frog-ging over opponents who've been at this much longer than you." Remy shrugged. "It's a gamble, but I'd bet on you."

It was a thought. On one hand, he didn't like the thought of using his connection to Daniel to help his career. On the other hand, butterflies stirred in his gut at the possibility of bringing Daniel home afterward.

Aden appeared in the doorway. "How's it going?"

Remy lit. Jealousy rocked Isaac on his feet. He'd never known their happiness.

"We're good. I take it Gunnar took over for a bit," Remy said, still smiling like an idiot.

Aden nodded. "Care to take a break with me?" Aden's

gaze hadn't wavered from his husband not once. Isaac couldn't stop staring.

"Sure. If Isaac doesn't need me, that is."

Aden crossed the room. "Isaac doesn't need you as much as I do," Aden said as he lowered his shoulder and tossed Remy over it. Remy's laughter filled the apartment. Isaac couldn't stop smiling, neither could he speak. Some people found what they had. Most didn't. Isaac was fine with being alone, but he couldn't pretend they weren't gorgeous.

Without looking back, Aden headed for the door with Remy slung over his shoulder. Isaac's feet moved, following them out. He didn't want to look away. Before that moment, Isaac hadn't thought he was missing anything. After making his way down the back steps, Aden didn't head back inside the building. Instead, he circled around the opposite side of the building. Isaac lost his excuse to keep following. He headed inside, swallowing down his disappointment over missing the rest of the show.

His discontent fell away the moment he stepped through the door. Daniel stood nearby with his back to the door. Isaac's mouth watered. He'd tasted that body. Isaac wanted it again. Before he'd fully made up his mind, Isaac was already closing the distance between them. Daniel turned. Their gazes met. The way Daniel's sexy mouth lifted at one corner said Isaac's interest was written all over his face.

"You're back."

Daniel dipped his chin, but his eyes never wavered from Isaac. "I am. There's not much to do in this town, so I thought I'd come back and watch some sparring."

"What about afterward?"

Daniel cocked his head as if he hadn't expected Isaac to make the first move. "I haven't decided."

They may as well have been touching. There was so much energy between them. "Maybe I could tempt—"

"We have a runner. I've got ten bucks on Remy. He's fast." The yell cut through the air and drew Isaac up short as everyone raced to the window. He turned to find Remy running top speed through the parking lot with Aden hot on his heels.

"You're on," someone behind him chimed in. "Remy might be quick, but Aden is determined."

"What the hell?" Isaac breathed.

A low chuckle escaped Daniel, brushing over Isaac's skin. Isaac fought the urge to close his eyes against the pleasure the sound brought. He glanced over, losing interest in whatever went on outside. Daniel turned his head, meeting Isaac's stare. His eyes swam with laughter. Isaac couldn't breathe.

"My money is on Aden too. He has a lot of incentive."

Isaac cleared his throat, trying to bring his breathing under control. "Is this a normal thing around here?"

Daniel snorted. "Always." He shrugged and went back to staring out the window. Isaac couldn't stop looking at him. The way his mouth quirked held Isaac captivated. A few hoots mixed with groans rent the air. "Oh, look," Daniel said in the driest tone Isaac had ever heard. "I should've put some real money on it."

Isaac turned his gaze away and focused on the pair outside. Remy was—once again—draped over Aden's shoulder. Even from where he stood, he could see Aden's triumphant smile and hear Remy's raucous laughter. Everyone scattered as they headed for the door. Without an ounce of shame, Aden strolled through the gym with Remy over his shoulder. He headed for his office and shut them inside.

"I need to get back to unpacking." Isaac heard the words as if they came from someone else. Seeing Remy and Aden together shone a light on something inside him. He didn't like what he saw. He didn't bother glancing Daniel's way. "Maybe I'll catch you before you leave." Isaac headed for the door without looking back. There was nothing there, but another man who only craved his body, and Isaac wanted nothing from anyone.

DANIEL WATCHED Isaac leave in a stunned silence. He'd been certain the man had been on the verge of offering something amazing for the evening. Then, the moment was gone. He mulled over the past few minutes, coming up blank. Daniel honestly didn't believe Isaac was playing some new game. He'd been straightforward in the past. With a shrug, he headed for Aden's office. His knuckles barely brushed the oak door. If they were otherwise engaged, he wasn't one to cock block. To his surprise, Aden called out.

"Aye."

Still, Daniel only poked his head in. Aden was in the middle of wrapping Remy's knuckles. "Damn. I hoped for a different show."

Remy glanced over and winked but didn't respond.

"Perv," Aden said under his breath.

Daniel shrugged and claimed an empty chair. "You say tomato. I say I love to watch."

"If you want a show, you should hang around. I'm about to hand Mateo's ass to him," Remy said, sounding confident. For good reason.

"I heard. Mateo invited me to stay and check him out in action."

Aden smoothed the tape over Remy's knuckles before slipping the first glove on. "How did the mock interview session go?"

Even though Aden wasn't looking at him, Daniel shrugged again. "Fine. He'll get eaten alive by the press if he wins a title... or he won't. In truth, he reminds me a little of Boston—too confident for his own good. The man tells everything he knows while thinking he's being slick. He thinks he's pulling the wool over my eyes and using me to his advantage, while the truth is I'm letting it happen because it fits with my agenda. That sort of thing."

Aden shook his head and helped Remy with his second glove. "Before Drew suggested this program, I never realized you were so ruthless." He flashed Daniel a smile. "I mean, I knew you were a little bastard, but I had no idea."

A smirk pulled at Daniel's lips. Aden really had no idea. If there was a line Daniel wouldn't cross, he hadn't found it yet. This life was his dream. He'd go to any length to be the best. "It's a gift."

Aden grunted. The sound could've meant anything. Daniel chose not to think too much on it. With Remy squared away, he kissed the tip of the man's nose and circled his desk. "Will you do me a favor?"

Daniel blinked for a moment, trying to decide if Aden spoke to him since he wasn't looking at him. Finally, Aden glanced up and met his gaze, as if waiting for Daniel's answer. He straightened in his seat. "Oh, you mean me. Sure."

The way Aden shook his head couldn't have screamed any louder that he thought Daniel was an idiot. Daniel didn't know what it was about Aden. He liked the guy, but he couldn't read the man at all. Aden could love him or hate him. Daniel would never know. Aden pulled a set of keys out of his desk drawer and held them out. "Isaac is opening the gym for me tomorrow. He grabbed the wrong keys when he was in here earlier. If you circle the building, you'll see a set of stairs. His apartment is up there. He's probably still unpacking. I'd take these to him, but Remy's match is starting soon and I'm afraid I'll forget if I wait."

Daniel accepted the keys. "It's no problem. Do you need me to get the other set of keys back?"

Aden shook his head. "Those are for the storage building out back. He might need those too."

Daniel stood, fighting back a triumphant smile. The universe kept handing him excuses to see Isaac. Who was he to turn his nose up at fate? "I'll take care of it."

"Thanks," Aden said, urging Remy toward the door. If Daniel wasn't mistaken, he would've sworn Remy flashed a knowing glance his way. The moment passed too quickly for Daniel to get a good grasp. He followed the pair from the office, biting back his anticipation. By the time he made it up the stairs, his hunger was full blown. An empty box flew out the open doorway, nearly taking Daniel's head off.

"Whoa. All you have to do is tell me I'm not welcome."

Isaac spun. "Holy shit. I didn't see you there."

"I should hope not," Daniel said on a laugh as he stepped through the door without an invitation. "Aden sent me up here with these," Daniel added, holding the keys out. "He says you grabbed the keys to the storage building earlier by mistake."

Isaac took them and tossed them on the kitchen counter. "Thanks for bringing them up here. How bad would it have sucked if I'd been locked out on my first day of opening the gym alone?"

Daniel took a look around. The place was bigger than he expected—open and tastefully decorated. "I can't imagine

Aden being too upset," Daniel said as he checked out each room without shame. The place had three bedrooms. Only one had furniture inside. The rest were bare. Several unopened boxes sat stacked in the eat-in area of the kitchen. "Would you like some help unpacking? It looks like you still have quite a ways to go."

"I have a hard time picturing you getting dirty," Isaac said, rather than answering.

"Do you?" Daniel asked. His gaze latched onto Isaac's. "Do you have a hard time picturing that?"

Isaac's gaze dropped to Daniel's mouth. Daniel's lips tingled beneath the man's stare. "Remy was helping me unpack dishes earlier, if you'd like to do that."

"I think I'd rather start in the bedroom," Daniel said. Without waiting to see Isaac's reaction or to get shut down, Daniel headed for the only room with a bed. In the middle of the bedroom, Daniel waited. There were unpacked boxes, but he didn't touch them. Instead, he held his breath. His ears strained. He heard the front door shut. Daniel could feel Isaac moving closer—like they were connected by some invisible force. Isaac's hands slid around Daniel's body. Daniel drew a slow breath through his nose, hoping to slow his heart.

"You should take this off," Isaac said against the shell of Daniel's ear as he slid Daniel's light-pink Polo higher. "It's too nice to ruin. Some of these boxes are dusty."

"I told Mateo I would watch him spar with Remy."

A low laugh caressed Daniel's ear. "You've been here five minutes, so you've probably already missed him get knocked the fuck out, but you're free to go," Isaac said, stepping back. He turned away before Daniel turned around.

Daniel overcame him. One arm encircled the man's

waist while his other hand tightened on Isaac's jaw. He held the man in place. Isaac's ass bumped Daniel's hardened cock. "I might be free to go, but you're not," Daniel growled, tilting Isaac's head back and biting his lobe. "I didn't come here for my health. I came for you," he said as he nipped his way down to where Isaac's neck and shoulder met. Daniel's hand slipped beneath Isaac's shirt. Damn, he loved the way the man's abs felt. His grip tightened on Isaac's jaw as he bit Isaac's shoulder. A desperate-sounding moan came from the back of Isaac's throat. He hated giving up Isaac's abs, but Daniel's hand slid lower. Isaac's hard dick stood proud, straining against the slick material of his pants. Daniel didn't hesitate to shove his hand inside, roughly palming Isaac's erection. Isaac moved against his touch as if he sought more. He fucking loved the way Isaac responded to the rough stuff.

Daniel had always been slightly twisted. He knew it. Didn't care what anyone thought. Hard sex was amazing. It was even better if it hurt a little. Isaac moaned like he knew. Daniel couldn't take it. He shoved Isaac's pants down and two-handed the man's dick. He squeezed and pulled while massaging his balls. The way Isaac's ass ground against Daniel's erection had him half insane. He'd gone too long ignoring his body's needs. Now he wanted to hear Isaac scream. He pumped fast as if Isaac's orgasm would be his when it hit. His finger sought and found Isaac's asshole. The man's cries were Daniel's guide. He shoved as many fingers inside as he could fit, fucking Isaac with both hands in any way he could.

Daniel's dick leaked inside his underwear, begging for its turn. At the rate they were going, Daniel wondered if the brush of his clothes would have him coming in his pants. The way they caressed his cock with every bump of Isaac's ass was torture. He wanted to set it free and shove himself deep inside Isaac.

Isaac cried out. Hot cum coated Daniel's fingers. Before the man's moans finished echoing from the walls, Daniel spun him around and shoved him to his knees. His dick was free and hitting the back of Isaac's throat before the cum on his fingers cooled. Isaac stared up the line of Daniel's body as he sucked him off. Daniel brought his fingers to his lips and licked away Isaac's cum as the man watched. Male salt coated his tongue. Isaac swirled his tongue around Daniel's crown, teasing him. He didn't know why they were such an inferno together, but they were. Only minutes in each other's company always turned into an explosion. Daniel caressed Isaac's jaw as he fucked the man's mouth. He wanted to slow the moment down and savor Isaac's talent. If he'd known the man sucked dick like this, he might've called every night. Isaac was dangerous. He made Daniel want to reward him.

"I've never seen a sexier man than you are right now." Even to Daniel's ears, he sounded turned on. "I still plan to fuck you," he promised before tightening his hold on the back of Isaac's neck and guiding him into the perfect rhythm. Isaac didn't wilt under the pace. If anything, Daniel's treatment seemed to arouse him. Isaac sucked harder and moans vibrated around Daniel's cock. The sounds sent tiny pops of electricity through Daniel. His balls drew up tight. The pressure built, climbing up his erection. He blew. Isaac's name tore from his throat, taking all the air from his lungs with it. Still, Isaac sucked and licked—like he couldn't stop or he'd die. He was killing Daniel. Daniel wanted that hot pull on his dick to last forever, but Isaac's asshole was even better. He tugged, urging Isaac to his feet. Once he was there, Daniel claimed his lips, tasting his own cum on the man's tongue.

"I should've called," Daniel admitted as he worked Isaac's shirt over his head and went after him from a different angle. Maybe he would next time. It seemed they had something that wasn't quite finished yet.

JUST LIKE THE last time they'd been together, Isaac couldn't begin to explain what happened. One second, he'd been unpacking. The next, he was on his knees and sucking Daniel's dick. Now Daniel was kissing him like he intended to stay. Isaac was just riding the high.

His hands shook. Isaac quivered from the inside out. Daniel touching him was two parts adrenaline and one part complete madness. Isaac never got excited about anything outside his career any longer. Daniel was the exception. They touched and Isaac lived in the moment, forgetting everything else. The apartment could be on fire and Isaac wasn't sure he'd notice. What was left of their clothes fell away as they fought to get closer.

"It won't be like last time," Daniel said between kisses. He urged Isaac back toward the bed. When the back of Isaac's knees hit the edge of the mattress, Daniel shoved, toppling Isaac onto his back. He stood over Isaac—nude and proud. "This time when I fuck you, you'll look me in the eye and chant my name as I take you."

Isaac's dick leaked on his stomach like he hadn't orgasmed only minutes earlier. He was so fucking horny, he could barely breathe past the lust tightening his throat. Daniel massaged Isaac's thighs and eyed him like he was staring at a feast. Isaac had never felt more powerful. "You're a beautiful man, Isaac." Daniel's praise was like fingers stroking Isaac's skin. His hands moved higher, urging Isaac's thighs apart as his touch moved closer to where Isaac wanted him most. Isaac's legs dangled off the bed. He fought the urge to pull his knees up, spread his ass cheeks, and beg for Daniel's cock. The edge of Daniel's thumb lightly brushed Isaac's balls. Isaac swallowed a moan at the contact.

"There's so much I want to do to you." Daniel's voice had gone rough, as if he could picture all the possibilities. With the barest of urging, Daniel had Isaac lifting his knee, giving the man access to all of him. "I want to watch as I finger you." That was all the warning Isaac got before Daniel pushed one finger past the ring of muscles surrounding his asshole. Isaac's body automatically tried pulling him deeper. Daniel's eyes fell closed for a moment. When they reopened, Isaac damn near swallowed his tongue at the heat radiating from Daniel's gaze. He'd never seen anyone look more aroused. "Your body is just begging for me to climb inside." Daniel pumped his finger inside Isaac's ass as he made the claim. "Are you fantasizing about my dick yet?" Daniel asked as he added a second finger to the mix.

Isaac fought not to writhe or tug on his cock to get relief. He pressed his hand to his stomach, trying to ease some of the tension coiling in his gut. "I've fantasized about your dick in my ass more in this past year than I care to admit."

Daniel's gaze sharpened. A third finger stretched his hole. "Is that so?" Daniel didn't wait for Isaac's answer. "Have you played with yourself and fucked your toys with my name on your lips?"

Isaac pressed harder on his stomach. He needed the deep thrusts. The stretching and pounding. "Yes." Even if Daniel had shown an ounce of triumph over the admission, Isaac would've been incapable of not admitting the truth.

Luckily, Daniel's expression never wavered, sparing Isaac's pride.

"Don't move from this spot."

Isaac didn't need to be told twice. He wasn't sure he as much as breathed when Daniel moved away. The man bent, digging through his pants and giving Isaac one hell of an amazing show. Daniel resurfaced with a condom. Isaac watched in breathless anticipation as Daniel rolled the condom down his erection. It was so goddamn sexy. Isaac wasn't sure he blinked.

"This is only the beginning."

A whimper escaped Isaac at Daniel's promise. He feared some form of fucked-up addicted madness waited around the bend. Isaac had never been this on edge. Daniel probed at Isaac's asshole. Isaac held his breath. Daniel massaged Isaac's cock as he pushed his way inside an inch before retreating. The tension had Isaac on the verge of cracking a tooth from clenching his jaw. In one quick thrust, Daniel impaled him. An orgasm slammed into Isaac without warning. Waves of ecstasy ripped through him. Jets of hot semen coated Isaac's skin. Daniel didn't slow. He thrust inside Isaac even as he leaned in and claimed Isaac's mouth. Mewling sounds came from the back of Isaac's throat even as he tried licking every inch of Daniel's tongue. Some sane corner of his brain wondered if he'd survive this intact. Isaac recognized how easily he could come to crave this insanity. He meant nothing to Daniel. Hell, Isaac wasn't sure Daniel meant anything to him. Still, it was almost frightening how explosive they were every time they saw each other—like they couldn't help themselves.

Daniel didn't lie. He didn't stop. One orgasm led to another. Light turned to darkness. Isaac forgot a world existed outside his bedroom. All he saw was Daniel. By the time midnight rolled around, Isaac was an exhausted heap, floating on a cloud. Several times, he dozed, startling himself awake each time his chin dropped. Movement from Daniel's side of the bed had his eyes popping open once more. As Isaac looked on, Daniel pulled his shirt over his head and grabbed his shoes. By his slow and careful movements, it couldn't have been more obvious he hoped to slip away without getting caught. Against his will, a laugh escaped Isaac. Daniel spun toward the bed. Even in the darkened room, Isaac could see the horror in Daniel's expression. Isaac put him out of his misery.

"You don't have to sneak away, babe."

"I wasn't sneaking."

At Daniel's response, Isaac hummed his disbelief. "Mhmm, okay. Seriously, though, my feelings won't be hurt if you don't want to stay."

Daniel moved to Isaac's side. He hovered over him. "I have a five-a.m. radio spot scheduled followed by a conference call. This isn't me sneaking. I know you're a big boy who doesn't expect more."

That might've stung if it hadn't been true. Isaac sat up and snagged Daniel's waist. "If there's a next time, you should definitely wake me up so I can offer a proper goodbye. I'd hate for your last memory of me to be you sneaking away."

"For fuck's sake."

Isaac hauled Daniel across his lap and captured the man's lips before he could say more. Damn, he hoped they ran into each other again. He'd done some crazy shit in his life, but no one had ever rocked him the way Daniel did. With one final nibble on Daniel's bottom lip, Isaac released him.

"See? Wasn't that better?"

"I concede your point," Daniel said, sounding breathless. "Go back to sleep," Daniel ordered as he disentangled himself. Isaac let him go and settled back down.

"When you climb into that uncomfortable hotel bed, think of me and what you lost."

Daniel's dark-sounding chuckle rumbled through the room. "When you wake up well rested because you didn't have me disturbing you at an ungodly hour in the morning, think of me."

"Fair enough," Isaac said, hearing the smile in his voice and incapable of hiding it. He liked Daniel. "See ya around."

"Yeah," Daniel said, sounding confident. "I'll lock the door on my way out." Isaac closed his eyes, the weight of exhaustion pulling him under. If Daniel said anything more, Isaac missed it. Daniel had wrung him dry.

4

———

"*You* missed my sparring session yesterday."

Daniel pasted on a fake smile to hide his irritation. He'd somehow managed to get through his mock interview session for the day without seeing Mateo. It seemed his good fortune wasn't holding. "I got sidetracked. Did you win?"

Mateo made a dismissive sound. "No one really wins or loses a sparring match. It's just practice."

He'd lost. Just as Isaac said he would. "I'm here for another two weeks. Maybe I'll catch you the next time."

"Or maybe I could take you to dinner tonight?"

This sucked. Thanks to agreeing to take part in Drew's special training program, he had to come here for work. Mateo's offer posed a problem Daniel didn't need. If he said no, there'd be hard feelings, but there was no way in hell he would say yes.

"Daniel, could I get your opinion on something?"

Daniel flashed Mateo an apologetic smile and turned away at the sound of Isaac's voice. His gaze never wavered from Isaac as he crossed the room. Isaac's expression remained closed, even once Daniel was at his side.

"You looked like you needed rescuing."

Daniel couldn't keep the relief from his voice. "Yes. Thank you." Isaac's bland expression gave him pause. "Although you don't look happy about saving me."

There was a shift in Isaac's eyes, and Daniel knew—he was laughing on the inside. "He's still watching you. I'm trying to look professional, since I'm sure you're hoping to avoid a nasty work entanglement." Isaac cocked his head to one side and seemed to think it over before adding, "Unless you want what Mateo is offering." There was a tiny part of Daniel that hoped to see Isaac's jealous side. He didn't get the chance. "Oops," Isaac said with a wince. "It didn't work. Here he comes. I tried."

Daniel glanced over his shoulder. Isaac was right. Mateo was closing in fast. "Jesus," Daniel said under his breath. He pulled his cell phone out and pretended to answer a fake ring. Daniel watched Isaac fighting back a smile. Damn, he'd tasted those lips—fucked them. Daniel regretted nothing. Mateo slowed when he spotted Daniel on his phone but didn't stop. Instead, he focused on Isaac. Daniel made an unsavory discovery. Mateo was a player. The man didn't care who he caught. He intended to drag the sea with his net. It didn't matter which fish he entangled first. He honestly hadn't needed another reason to be turned off by Mateo, but there it was.

"That's unfortunate," Daniel said, playing his comments off as part of his phone conversation. It really was bad luck for Mateo. For the next two weeks, Isaac already had more man than he could handle.

Isaac shot him a knowing gaze before focusing on

Mateo. "What's up, man? How'd your sparring match go with Remy yesterday?"

Mateo's entire demeanor matched a man on the make—from his slimy smile to his way he held his shoulders. "It was a learning experience, which was the point, of course. But I was actually hoping I could convince you to slip on the gloves today and meet me in the ring."

"I'll call you back," Daniel said, putting an end to his fake call. This, he needed to see. He sidled closer, inserting himself in the conversation. "Did I overhear something about a sparring match between you two?"

Mateo's practiced smile flashed Daniel's way. "Yeah. I'm trying to convince Isaac to step in the ring with me. From what I hear, he gave Gregor McCully a proper beat down a few weeks ago."

Daniel hadn't heard that, but he couldn't watch every level of each sport all the time. He switched his attention to Isaac. "You beat McCully?" It was no wonder he'd moved here, then. That put Isaac light years ahead of other boxers to challenge for the Super Middleweight title.

Isaac shrugged. "It's no big deal. I got lucky."

A snort escaped Daniel. "No big... are you insane or being modest?"

Isaac shifted from foot to foot, looking uncomfortable. He'd never seen the man react in such a way, and Daniel had definitely put Isaac in some uncomfortable positions. Isaac's gaze swept the room, as if he searched for an escape. "If you give me a few minutes to tape up, I'll spar," Isaac finally said, making Daniel wonder if Isaac would rather do anything at all other than discuss his win. Proving him right, Isaac walked away, leaving Daniel staring after him.

Daniel focused on Mateo. "So he really beat McCully?"

Mateo nodded. "By knockout."

"Yet you want to step in the ring with him?" Daniel asked, incapable of keeping the disbelief from his voice. He knew Mateo was good, but Isaac had twenty pounds on Mateo, which might not seem like much, but it mattered a whole hell of a lot in the ring. Not to mention, the man had gotten his ass handed to him by Remy. Granted, Remy was a former champion, but Remy was smaller than Mateo.

The smirk shaping Mateo's lips gave Daniel a chill, and not in a good way. "You know he fought the MMA circuit for years before this, right? I totally want him to show me his every move. MMA fighters have fantastic hip control."

Wow. Just when Daniel thought he couldn't hate the dude more, Mateo would open his mouth again. Daniel switched his gaze to where Isaac stood, talking to Remy. Immediately, the tightness in his gut eased. Isaac wasn't like most people. He might be a sexual powerhouse, but he didn't carry himself the same as the Mateos of the world. It was refreshing. The silence coming from Mateo struck Daniel as odd. He snuck a peek the man's way. There was something unnamed in the man's gaze before Mateo caught Daniel staring and masked it behind a predatory smile. Daniel went back to watching Isaac as he mused over what he'd seen. He'd have to look into Mateo's life. There was something there. Daniel loved a good mystery.

Remy looked their way and motioned for them to join Isaac and him. As one, they moved to the men's sides. Remy was oddly serious as he eyed each of them. "Mateo, I understand you want to schedule some ring time with Isaac."

Even though it hadn't been a question, Mateo treated it as one. "Yes. Despite our different weight class, I'm always up for some practice time."

Remy nodded. "Isaac says he's willing, but it'll have to wait until next week. You know the rules around here. Ring time is on rotation. Not to mention, Isaac is on the clock and I have things for him to do. Right now, Daniel, Aden's office is open if you'd like to go ahead and do Josef's mock interview. That'll free up Friday for you."

Daniel blinked. "Do I need Friday free?"

"Yes," Remy said, as if Daniel had no say so in the matter. "You'll be in Miami with us for Friday night fights."

"Who is us?" Daniel wasn't trying to be a dick. He was genuinely curious where this was headed.

"Aden, Isaac, and me." Remy switched his gaze to Isaac. "Do you mind straightening out the weights section? These guys, I love them, but they're messy as fuck."

Isaac nodded. "No problem." He headed off to do Remy's bidding without a backward glance. Daniel desperately wanted to watch him go, but he was too focused on the way Mateo's gaze followed Isaac's every move. It seemed he wasn't the only one. Remy's eyes were narrowed on the man. His face cleared when Mateo turned his head and focused on Remy. The entire situation had Daniel's curiosity eating him alive.

"Can I help with anything, Remy?"

At Mateo's question, Daniel somehow managed to stare harder at the man's features. Mateo's voice had changed. He sounded softer—like he was an actual human. The muscles in Daniel's shoulders tightened. A rock landed in his gut. This wasn't good.

Remy winked. "You're good, Mateo. Just go finish your workout." He started to turn away before obviously remembering why they were standing there in the first place. "Oh, yeah. Don't forget to put your name on the list for ring time next week."

"Of course." The silky note to Mateo's tone had chills racing down Daniel's spine, and not the good kind. With a wink for Daniel, Mateo walked away. Before he could stop himself, Daniel grabbed Remy's elbow and steered the man toward Aden's office. Remy didn't argue. Thank god. He didn't consider all the many ways Aden would kill him for manhandling Remy until it was too late.

The instant they were alone, he turned on Remy. "That guy is trouble."

"Which one?" Remy didn't sound unconcerned, merely confused.

"Mateo. I'm telling you, you need to keep an eye on him. I can't explain it. It's just a gut feeling. You should leave his training and sparring to someone else."

Remy turned and closed the door before focusing on Daniel once more. "Okay. What's going on?"

Daniel shrugged, feeling useless. "I just need you to believe me. Okay? I'm a damn good judge of character, and something about him... I don't know. It's just not right."

"Okay. It won't be hard for me to find excuses since I rarely spar any longer. Now." Remy slapped his hands together. His demeanor changed, transforming into the version of Remy people found irresistible. "So, Friday night? Are you in?"

Daniel's shoulders sagged under the relief of Remy believing him. "Of course. Just tell me when and where."

"Meet us out front at eight. Nothing really gets going until around ten."

Now that the panic inside him ebbed, Daniel was hooked on this new topic. "Why am I going to local fights with you?"

Remy's green gaze flashed with mischief. "Do you have something better to do with your time?"

"No," Daniel said, dragging out the word. "But I'm getting a vibe—like you're up to no good."

A mock gasp of outrage escaped Remy. His expression immediately shifted into that of a naughty child. "You caught me. I'm totally up to something. Give me a boost up, will ya?" he said, pushing his way past Daniel. "I'm about to tack this Photoshopped picture of Aden with Ariel Craymore up in the corner. Want to put some money on how long it takes him to notice it?"

"Who is Ariel Craymore?" Daniel asked as he helped Remy climb onto a cabinet in the corner and held on so the man wouldn't fall.

"She's a teenage pop singer he hates with a passion. He mutters obscenities under his breath anytime her name is mentioned. Speaking of which," Remy added, smiling over his shoulder. "You should definitely start thinking up ways to throw her name into every conversation."

Daniel's face hurt from smiling already, and he'd been in Remy's company less than ten minutes. "You get that Aden really is the luckiest bastard on the planet, right?"

Remy used a thumbtack to hang the pic before hopping back down to the floor. He flashed Daniel a sweet smile. "Not really. I'm the lucky one. You get that I'm an obnoxious ass, right? Aden's the only person who's ever spent more than a week in my company and hasn't wanted to kill me." He winced. "I'm not for everyone."

"Well, you should be," Daniel said, experiencing an overwhelming desire to pat Remy on the head—like a little brother. "I think you're awesome. This isn't me hitting on you," Daniel tacked on, because he knew how all this sounded.

To his surprise, a bright smile lit Remy's face. "I know. You're a good guy, Daniel. That's why we keep you around." Remy headed for the door. He paused and looked back before opening it. "Plus, I think someone else we know has caught your eye, and I approve. So, should I send Josef in?" Remy asked, not giving Daniel time to react to his revelation.

Daniel chose to let it ride. "Sure. Send him in." It wasn't as if he could deny Isaac had his attention. Not to mention, Remy had set up a date with the man for Friday night. Daniel couldn't deny, he kind of liked it here.

For Isaac, his day was one part avoiding Mateo and one part trying not to stare at Daniel. By the time he circled the building and headed up to his apartment, his brain was fried from the effort. One hot shower later and Isaac was somewhat closer to human. Beads of water still clung to his skin, and a towel was wrapped around his waist when a knock landed on his door. He already saw the problem with living above the gym. Everyone knew he lived there. Stowing his irritation, he answered.

Daniel stood on the other side, holding some grocery bags. Isaac's nose tingled like he'd been drinking champagne. That was how ridiculously happy seeing Isaac made him. Daniel's gaze swept over Isaac's body.

"Mhmm. Goddamn."

Isaac had to take a breath at Daniel's appraisal. Without a word, he stepped aside, inviting Daniel inside.

"I brought food," Daniel said over his shoulder as he carried the bags to the counter. "I'm not a great cook, since I rarely do it, but this fucking town has nothing. Don't get me wrong, it's beautiful here, but who—" Isaac overcame him, crushing the man against the counter and cutting off his words. He encircled Daniel's waist and pressed his lips to the man's nape. The air stuttering from the back of Daniel's throat sounded as loud as gunfire. The thin towel did nothing to hide Isaac's erection.

"It's been hard watching you all day and not doing this."

"That would've turned some heads," Daniel said, sounding breathless.

"Yeah, and I need my job," Isaac said as he trailed kisses down the side of Daniel's neck.

"You also need food." Even as Daniel made the claim, he reached behind him and massaged Isaac's cock.

Isaac popped the button on Daniel's pants. "You're right. I do." With the slightest urging, he had Daniel turned in his arms. Their mouths clashed. Isaac worked at setting Daniel's erection free. He fisted and stroked until Daniel moved against his hand, openly seeking relief. Once he had Daniel mindless, Isaac dropped to his knees. He swallowed Daniel's dick, reveling in the man's cries. His knees dug into the hard kitchen floor. Isaac ignored the pain. He jacked off as he sucked Daniel's dick—licking and taking the man down his throat. Isaac followed Daniel's moans, using them as his guide. Every time Daniel's muscles tensed and his breathing deepened, Isaac backed off and tightened his hold on Daniel's cock, choking off his orgasm.

Daniel's short fingernails scraped at the back of Isaac's neck as he tried taking what he wanted. A growl reverberated off the walls of the kitchen. "Quit teasing," Daniel ordered, sounding beyond frustrated.

"Trust me," Isaac begged. He toyed with Daniel's crown, purposefully driving the man insane before hollowing out his cheeks and taking Daniel deep. This time, when Daniel tensed, Isaac increased his pace. Daniel's cock sawed in and out of his mouth, slamming against the back of Isaac's throat. Isaac pumped his own dick faster, letting the pressure build. Daniel's pleasure was his. Isaac exploded. He sucked hard. Hot cum filled his mouth even as it coated his fingers. Isaac moaned around Daniel's cock. Daniel's fingers dug into Isaac's shoulders as he fought to stay upright beneath Isaac's ministrations. Isaac didn't stop licking and swallowing until Daniel begged for mercy.

"I guess it's a lucky thing you had a towel," Daniel breathed out on a chuckle.

"It's almost like I planned it," Isaac agreed as he cleaned up their mess and came to his feet. For a moment, they stared at one another. They had a connection. It was a tug at the center of Isaac's chest. Maybe this would go somewhere. Chances were, it wouldn't. That didn't stop Isaac from slowly lowering his head, as if daring Daniel to deny there wasn't something between them, before touching his lips to Daniel's. Neither man attempted to deepen their kiss. They clung to each other as if memorizing the sensations of their lips brushing. Daniel was the first to touch his tongue to Isaac's bottom lip, tracing the seam and seeking entrance. Isaac couldn't explain why it felt like a win.

5

*F*riday night came too slow yet too fast for Daniel's peace of mind. It was a week down and one more to go. He couldn't decide if he was looking at the glass half empty or half full. One full week in Isaac's company, and it had been the most amazing week of his life. Unfortunately, it marked the loss of a week in Isaac's company. Soon, he'd be on the road again. All of this would be a memory. He couldn't stop staring at the jeans stretching across Isaac's sexy ass. They were too baggy in the waist, but the man's thighs were so massive, he couldn't possibly wear a smaller size. It was incredibly fucking hot.

"Aden and Remy are supposed to meet us out front in ten minutes."

Daniel tore his gaze away from Isaac's ass and forced himself to meet the man's stare. "I guess we should head down, then," Daniel suggested. He considered pushing himself from the couch and heading for the door. The intense way Isaac watched his every move had Daniel frozen in place and wishing they hadn't agreed to go to Miami. He had one week left with Isaac. It wasn't anywhere near enough time. As Daniel looked on, Isaac crossed the room. Daniel couldn't tear his gaze away. His breathing deepened. His dick hardened. How one person could control his body with only a look was a complete mystery to Daniel.

"We'll go in a minute. Let me do this first," Isaac said, leaning down and capturing Daniel's lips. He straddled Daniel's hips, pinning him to the couch. Their tongues entwined. Daniel was ready to head for the bedroom. Fuck going to Miami. It would still be there next Friday night. Without a second thought, Daniel kneaded Isaac's cock through his jeans, hoping to tempt him to stay. One day soon, Daniel would be back in New York. All this would be over. He needed some memories to take to bed with him at night. Isaac's pants vibrated.

Daniel pulled away. He dropped his gaze to Isaac's crotch. "That's new."

With a chuckle, Isaac shifted positions and pulled his phone from inside his pocket. "Text message," he said, flashing Daniel a smile. Isaac checked his messages. He rolled his eyes, and Daniel made an odd discovery—even the man's childish gesture was sexy as fuck. He tossed the phone aside and met Daniel's stare. "I get the feeling we've been set up."

Daniel massaged Isaac's thighs, unrealistically content having the man straddling his lap. "How so?"

"That was Remy, saying they wouldn't be able to make it tonight, but we should go on without them."

Daniel's eyebrows rose. "Matchmaking?"

Isaac smiled. "That's my guess."

As if his hands had a mind of their own, they slid higher up Isaac's thighs before circling his body and massaging his ass. "If they only knew what we were doing right now."

"I think we have to go to the matches or we'll have to tell them why we didn't."

Daniel thought it over. He was happier here with Isaac than he'd been in a long time, but he wasn't ready to share this with anyone. It would taint it somehow—like he'd have to share Isaac. Right now, he felt like they were alone in the world. Isolated. As things stood, either of them could walk away without having to offer explanations. They were something only for themselves. "I guess you're right."

"But we don't have to leave right this second." The hopeful note to Isaac's voice almost tempted him to stay.

Instead, Daniel sat forward. "Yes, we do. Once I get started, I don't want to stop. Let's see your match and then you'll be mine."

With a sigh that sounded a lot like regret, Isaac slid from Daniel's lap. "I'm holding you to that."

"You're on," Daniel said, not hesitating in his agreement. Isaac was a rare find—sexy, strong, and obedient in bed. He was the kind of man Daniel could play with forever.

It should've only taken an hour to get to the arena where the fights were being held. Miami traffic dragged things out to closer to two. They made it to their seats just in time to see the main fighters for the evening, climbing into the ring.

Isaac nodded toward the man in the center of the ring. "Aden says this guy is who I have to beat if I want to challenge Winston Raines for the Super Middleweight title."

Daniel eyed the mocha-skinned chiseled-jawed man in red shorts. He danced around the ring, pumping up the crowd with his charisma. In fact, the man's upbeat personality was one of the reasons Jericho Williams had such a huge following. Isaac needed to do more than beat Jericho. He needed to find a way to match the man's following. "Beating him might be the easy part."

Isaac glanced over. Daniel forgot what they were talking about the instant their gazes met. "What's that supposed to mean?"

Daniel searched his mind, digging out their conversation and getting back on track. "If you want people to chant your name, you have to give them a reason other than winning. See how he interacts with the crowd?" Isaac focused on the ring while Daniel kept his gaze locked on Isaac. "He makes people want to cheer for him—bet on him."

A wince crossed Isaac's features. "I'm not very likable. I'm more of a show-up-and-get-my-job-done sort of guy."

He could see that. Isaac was straightforward and genuine. Those were qualities Daniel adored. Most people couldn't give two shits about honesty. The vast majority of people craved drama, and fake people brought a lot of that bullshit to the table. Jericho was the perfect example. In reality, the man was as boring as watching golf on TV. He had no sense of humor to speak of. The dude chatted stats and talked about his meal planning like most people talked about their kids—with a hint of pride and love. It was freaky.

"You don't need his fake charisma," Daniel reassured him. "You just need to give them an excuse to root for you. It'll happen." At his claim, Isaac glanced over once more. Something stirred in Daniel's chest. He couldn't stop himself from adding, "After all, I'd cheer for you over anyone else."

Isaac's lips parted as if he wanted to say something but Daniel had confused the fuck out of him. Daniel couldn't look away. He wished he could hear Isaac's thoughts. The bell rang. A disappointed sigh reverberated off the walls of Daniel's mind. He expected the moment to end. Isaac didn't look away. Daniel couldn't either. "I'll miss you when you go back to New York."

It was Daniel's turn to be shocked speechless. He'd never expected Isaac to say anything remotely caring. Not because Isaac wasn't the type, but because Daniel wasn't worth it. One day soon, Isaac would figure that out. Daniel dreaded that moment. Until then, he intended to soak up as much goodness as he could. Life rarely threw people like Isaac his way.

———

SPENDING the evening with Daniel had been even better than Isaac could've imagined. At the arena, Daniel was in his element. He knew everything about everything. He'd spent the whole night, speaking against Isaac's ear, giving him tips and stats. It was a lesson he might've gotten from Aden—if the man had shown up, but it was better coming from Daniel. From him, it didn't feel like he'd been learning. They were almost back to Isaac's apartment. The dark and silence tricked Isaac's brain into thinking they were the only two people in the world. Each passing minute in Daniel's company brought Isaac closer to him.

"I have to be honest, I don't know how you stand living here, especially coming from Vegas," Daniel said, breaking the silence.

It didn't surprise Isaac that someone like Daniel would find the slow pace of the upper Keys boring. "It has its perks," Isaac said on a laugh.

Daniel was quiet long enough that Isaac cast a quick glance his way. He was turned sideways in his seat, watching Isaac drive. "You're here, so it's not a total loss," Daniel said, as if he'd been waiting for Isaac to look his way.

"There's also the ocean," Isaac reminded him while trying not to sound as pleased as he was by Daniel's words.

Daniel snorted. "There're sharks in the ocean. I'll pass."

"You don't have to get in it," Isaac said, trying to win Daniel to his side. "It's peaceful to look at. Here," he said, pulling to the side of the road before backing his way in closer to the edge of the water. "Let me give you the personal experience." Without waiting for Daniel's agreement, he hopped from the SUV. After circling the vehicle, he popped the hatch and climbed inside before lowering the back seats to give them as much room as possible.

Daniel was a little slower to follow. Finally, he appeared at the opening. "What are you doing?"

Isaac waved him inside. "Come on. I'm forcing the slow life on you." While openly wearing a puzzled expression, Daniel crawled into the back with Isaac. Isaac dug around until he came out with a stack of blankets. "The upside to not getting all my shit moved in yet is this," he said, stacking the covers to make a comfortable place for them to relax. He settled in and motioned for Daniel to join him. Daniel moved closer and settled into Isaac's arms. Isaac released a contented sigh. "See? It's not as boring as you think."

"Your tactics might be considered cheating, since most people aren't getting this experience." Despite his continued arguing, Daniel's body relaxed against Isaac's. He felt the tension drain from Daniel. Silence fell between them. It was comfortable—like they were meant for this moment. Daniel's hands landed on Isaac's arms around his waist. His fingers trailed from Isaac's wrist to his elbow and back again, threatening to put Isaac to sleep.

The sky was beautiful with its explosion of stars. In Vegas, he'd never seen a sky like this. It confused him—

made the moment seem more intimate than it likely was. "Can I tell you a secret?"

"I love secrets." The smile in Daniel's voice had Isaac smiling as well.

"I gave up everything to come here. All my family is in Vegas. It's the only home I've ever known. My mom works as a blackjack dealer at one of the casinos. My dad is a cop and my older brother works security at the same casino as my mom. I just walked away, leaving it all behind, and the truth is—I don't even care if I win a title."

"Then why did you give up everything and come here?"

Daniel's fingers continued trailing down Isaac's arm, making him feel like they were alone in the world. Their imagined familiarity in that moment had him confessing more than he should. "I don't want my life to be pointless."

Daniel shifted until he could meet Isaac's gaze. "Why would you think that it is?"

With a shrug, Isaac grabbed Daniel's hand and brought it to his lips. He held it there, kissing him while he thought of a way to explain something he never had before. "I was never all that great at MMA."

"Drew thought so."

A chuckle escaped Isaac at Daniel's observation. "Drew can be pretty biased when he likes someone. I mean, I won more matches than I lost, but I would've never held a title. I'm better at this. There's a real possibility people might know my name one day. I just don't have anything else, I guess."

"How do you mean?"

Isaac shrugged again. "I don't know how to explain it. Most people live mediocre lives, and it doesn't matter to them, because they go home every night to people who make them feel extraordinary. I don't have that. When I die, my life will have been pointless."

"We're a lot alike," Daniel said, sounding more like the comment had been meant for himself than Isaac.

Isaac scoffed. "That's not true. You're a roaring success at what you do. In Vegas, I never really got off the ground. Here, I'm living off Aden and Remy's charity while hoping for a miracle."

Daniel made a humming noise that sounded suspiciously like disbelief. "Actually, I meant we both obsess over things that are mostly all in our heads. You don't know Aden very well if you think he's a charitable person, and Drew— while he might be biased—doesn't like having his time wasted. Neither man would fuck with you at all if they didn't believe in you. I'm not downplaying your feelings, but—for what it's worth—I think you're better than you give yourself credit for being. I doubt you've ever had a mediocre moment in your life." There was so much passion in Daniel's voice— like he believed every word he said. Isaac was speechless. Coming up on his knees, Isaac leaned in, giving Daniel time to reject him. "Things aren't feeling the least bit unexceptional right now," Isaac admitted before touching his lips to Daniel's. For a moment, they simply shared each other's air as Isaac maneuvered Daniel onto his back and covered the man's body with his. As soon as he had Daniel pinned beneath him, Isaac deepened their kiss.

If Isaac knew one thing, it was that he shouldn't fool himself into thinking he was special to Daniel. The problem was—he already had. Sometimes, Daniel said the most amazing things, making Isaac feel like he mattered. He could never let the man find out. This was a temporary slice out of time. Daniel's world was everywhere but here. Isaac would never be the anchor, holding him back.

6

The two weeks Daniel had spent with Isaac had been the best weeks of Daniel's life. He'd been to New York and Oklahoma in the past week before finding his way back to Key Largo. He wasn't one to lie to himself. Daniel was there for Isaac because he also wasn't one to deny himself either.

"All the Vegas hopefuls left last Friday. Why are you back?" Aden asked the moment Daniel stepped inside his office.

Daniel refused to take the bait. Instead, he claimed the chair on the other side of Aden's desk and chose to change the subject. "I hear Ariel Craymore is coming to Miami in August. If you'd like, I can get you tickets for cheap." It was the best he could come up with, considering his brain was a mess. Since the picture Remy had hung in the corner was still there, Daniel wouldn't miss his chance to torment Aden.

Aden didn't look up from his paperwork. "You can drop the act. I'm fully aware there's a picture of Ariel and me hanging in the corner. I also clearly remember asking you why you're here a week after the hopefuls have all gone."

Daniel's smile fell. "Aren't you one to suck the fun from everything?" he said, still dodging. "Why haven't you taken it down?"

Aden flipped to the next page. "Remy doesn't know I know, and he's enjoying his joke. Not to mention, there's a pool going on when I'll notice. I gave Isaac two hundred dollars to put on July fourteenth. That's exactly when I intend to notice." He glanced up and winked. "We're going to split the profit."

"Evil bastard," Daniel said on a chuckle.

Aden shrugged and went back to staring at the pages spread across his desk. "I figure I've earned it for all the times I've had to listen to people say that dreadful girl's name."

"Where is Isaac today? I didn't see him out there."

"That's another act you can drop," Aden said, sounding bored. "I know you're sleeping together or dating. Whatever."

Daniel intentionally held his silence until Aden looked up. The moment their gazes met, Daniel held his stare, ensuring Aden saw how seriously he took the matter. "I don't hide. The fact that I'm seeing Isaac isn't a secret. I was simply inquiring where he is."

"I sent him to the store," Aden answered before getting back to work and leaving Daniel—once again—staring at the top of his head. "By the way, I'm glad you're not hiding. Isaac is a good guy. Don't destroy his reputation when you get bored and move on."

Daniel tried taking a breath before responding. He didn't want any problems with Aden, but he didn't succeed in checking his temper. "Wow. That was a dick thing to say."

Aden set his pen aside and focused on Daniel. "Are you saying I'm wrong?"

"Yeah," Daniel said, incapable of hiding his ire. "I've dated a lot of professional athletes in my career. Several, most people don't even know are gay. Not once have I used my position to harm anyone's reputation. If anything, I've been used by several people, hoping I would make them look good in the media, but I guess how I feel doesn't count."

Aden opened his mouth. Daniel didn't know what the man meant to say. It didn't matter. Daniel didn't care to hear it. He held up his hand, stopping Aden. "Save it," Daniel said, coming to his feet. "Please let Isaac know I stopped by."

"Daniel."

Daniel didn't slow at the sound of Aden calling his name. He'd already been in one of his moods when he'd stopped by. That was why he'd hopped a flight to come here with no notice. Daniel had hoped seeing Isaac would jar him from the blackness threatening to swallow him, but it seemed liquor would have to do instead.

ADEN STARED INTO SPACE, looking as if his thoughts had taken over, rendering him useless. Isaac waved a hand in front of his face. "Are you in there?"

Aden blinked. "Aye. How did it go?"

Isaac claimed the seat across from him. "Great. If you're determined to throw an all red birthday party for Remy, I've got you covered. I'm talking red velvet cake with red cream cheese icing. Red cups, plates, and dinnerware. I even picked up some red drink mix just to be on the safe side. Oh, and all red balloons, of course. I dropped everything off at your house." It had been a long morning, driving all over town to find the perfect everything for Remy's birthday party. Isaac didn't mind. It would all be worth it.

Aden nodded his approval. "That's great. Thank you. I should give you a raise."

Isaac waved off his words. "Absolutely not. You already pay me more than I deserve, especially on top of everything else you do for me."

The man scowled too much for Isaac's comfort. When he'd left to get the stuff for Remy's party, Aden had been smiling and practically rubbing his hands together at the idea of doing something special for Remy. Now it was obvious Aden's mood had gone to shit. "Are you okay?"

Aden leaned back in his chair and stared Isaac down as he rubbed at his bottom lip. Isaac didn't care for the inspection. He was certain he hadn't done anything wrong, but that didn't stop the discomfort from crawling up his spine.

"I've been thinking about your list of upcoming fights," Aden said, ignoring Isaac's question. "You should ask Daniel to write an article about you. Good press could get you moving along."

"No," Isaac said, surprising even himself by the growl in his tone. He tried toning it down. "I won't use my connection to Daniel to boost my career. That's his job. He worked hard to get where he is. I'd rather he not write about me."

Aden didn't budge. "If you win a title, he'll have to write about you. His boss will make sure of it."

"If his boss demands it, that's one thing. Otherwise, I don't want it."

Aden sat forward. "That's too bad. He came by here looking for you earlier. If you'd been interested in trying to get him to publish something, I might've sent you home early to hunt him down."

"He was here?" Isaac couldn't contain his smile. It tugged at his lips, making his cheeks ache. He tried pressing his lips together to no avail.

Aden eyed him as if searching for something. He sighed. "Fuck it. You've worked hard today. I think you should get out of here. As a matter of fact, I might throw all these fuckers out and corner Remy. It's been a long time since we fucked on this desk."

Isaac's gaze dropped to the aforementioned slab of wood separating them. His smile still wouldn't abate. He stood. "Thank you and remind me never to touch that desk again."

A loud snort filled the air. "Don't act like a prude, Isaac. You're not fooling anyone."

As if it were possible, Isaac's smile grew. "Yes, sir. I'll see you later." He fled before Aden changed his mind. The moment he was out of sight, Isaac pulled his phone from his back pocket and sent Daniel a text.

Isaac: *I hear you're in town **hopeful face***

Daniel: *Odyssey hotel room 261*

Isaac: *On my way ASAP*

Isaac ran upstairs for a quick shower before heading out to see Daniel. His excitement and happiness over getting to see a man he hadn't expected to see again was the only excuse he could muster for how shocked he was at the first sight of Daniel. He looked like Hell. Daniel never looked anything other than perfect. With his hair standing on end, as if he'd been running his fingers through it, Daniel blinked at Isaac as if he hadn't told him where he could be found.

Isaac eyed the wrinkled t-shirt Daniel wore before switching his gaze to the bottle of Jack the man held. "Um. Is everything okay?"

"Yeah," Daniel said, taking a step back and letting Isaac inside.

Isaac didn't let it go. "Are you sure? Because everything doesn't look okay."

Daniel closed the door behind Isaac before responding. "There's nothing wrong. I just get like this sometimes." After setting his bottle of liquor aside, Daniel moved to the bed and fell facedown across it.

"Get like what? Drunk?"

Daniel's answer came out sounding muffled by the mattress. "Like the inside of my head has been painted black. Don't worry. It'll pass."

Without a qualm, Isaac kicked off his shoes and climbed onto the bed. With his weight braced on his hands and knees, Isaac crawled up Daniel's body, kissing every bump of the man's spine along the way. When he reached Daniel's neck, Isaac pressed his lips to the spot beneath Daniel's ear. "Tell me what would make you happy."

Daniel shifted, as if to roll over. Isaac lifted, giving him space to do so. Moving with the speed of a sober man, Daniel's hand shot out, grabbing Isaac's throat and pulling him down. His grip loosened when their tongues met, but he didn't release Isaac. He couldn't remember the last time anyone held his throat the way Daniel did. Isaac's cock leaked inside his jeans. An image of riding Daniel's dick while Daniel held tight to his throat floated across Isaac's brain. He wanted it. Unfortunately, Isaac got the feeling Daniel's black mood needed something lighter.

He pulled away and kissed Daniel's jaw. "We should blare some music and have a dance party."

Rather than laughing, Daniel's grip tightened again. "You should take your clothes off and ride my dick."

Sitting back on his heels, Isaac tugged his shirt over his head and tossed it aside. Daniel worked on the button of Isaac's pants while Isaac made his job harder by trying to work Daniel's shirt up and over his head.

"Pants off," Daniel growled, proving his patience was nonexistent.

Isaac shifted positions, managing to wiggle out of his jeans and underwear. The instant he was bare assed, Daniel sat up and snagged Isaac's waist, hauling him higher as he settled back onto the mattress.

"I want you to fuck my mouth," Daniel said, sounding determined.

Isaac moved higher, holding on to the headboard to keep his balance as he straddled the man's head. Daniel didn't waste time. He sucked Isaac's balls and tongued his asshole. Dropping his chin, Isaac stared down the line of his body. Daniel's face was hard with lust. Isaac's hips moved of their own accord. He couldn't stop himself from fucking Daniel's mouth. The angle wasn't the best. Twice, Daniel gagged but didn't slow. Isaac couldn't tear his gaze away. He didn't know what was going on with Daniel tonight, but Isaac wanted to wipe away the rage. He needed to make Daniel smile and moan the way Daniel always did for him. Isaac's body screamed with pleasure. Daniel finger fucked Isaac's asshole as he licked Isaac's cock from crown to root before sucking his balls and starting the process over again. The build was slow. Isaac pumped against Daniel's lips, letting the ache grow. He never wanted the moment to end. When he couldn't take it another second, Isaac pulled away, fisted his cock, and jacked off until cum hit Daniel's cheek.

Daniel's eyes fell closed. He looked more turned on than any man should. Butterflies stirred in Isaac's gut as he stared down at Daniel. His body was on fire. His brain was a plea-sure-filled mess. With no plan in mind, Isaac shifted lower. He licked at Daniel's mouth and cheek, licking away his cum before capturing the man's mouth. He needed to taste his own juices on Daniel's tongue. Daniel's dick probed at Isaac's asshole as they kissed. It burned as Daniel pushed his way inside. He loved it. Craved it.

Turning his head, Isaac sucked a deep breath in through his mouth as Daniel stretched him wide and went deep. "Yes. God. Please."

"Look at me," Daniel demanded. His voice sounded almost demonic. Isaac turned his head. Their gazes met. Daniel surged upward, impaling Isaac. "You should stay away from me." Even as Daniel made the claim, he fucked Isaac's ass.

Isaac didn't hesitate. "No."

Daniel held Isaac still. "You'll regret me."

"I don't care," Isaac swore before rocking his hips and riding Daniel's dick while holding the man's stare.

Daniel cupped Isaac's face. His eyes looked sad, even with his flushed cheeks telling a different story. "Being with me is never free. Don't hate me when the check comes due."

Isaac froze. They stared at each other. The rest of the world disappeared. "Tell me," Isaac breathed. "I can take it."

For a moment, Isaac was certain Daniel was on the verge of baring his soul. Instead, he shook his head. "It's the alcohol talking. I just want to fly."

Isaac could do that. He could make Daniel feel like he was the only man in the world. Slowing things down, he kissed Daniel while rocking against him. He measured each movement, keeping a snail's pace while savoring Daniel's tongue. The way Daniel accepted the torturously slow love-making was intoxicating. The man screwed with Isaac's feelings.

Daniel tore his mouth away and pressed his lips to Isaac's ear. "When this is over, you'll sit in that chair over there and play with yourself until I tell you to stop. I don't care how many times you come, you'll tug on your dick and finger your hole until you're hard again, and you will not stop until you're told."

Isaac couldn't breathe beneath the image Daniel created. This man would be death of him. He couldn't think of a better way to go.

THE ROOM DIDN'T SPIN any longer, but the exhaustion was real. Daniel could barely lift his head from the pillow. That didn't stop him from staring at Isaac while he slept. Life was rarely peaceful for Daniel. He wasn't complaining. There was nothing he'd rather be doing. But this was amazing too. He'd never expected to meet someone like Isaac. This hadn't been in his plans. Isaac rolled from his side to his back before slinging his arm over his eyes. Daniel wanted his toy back. He didn't want to stop staring at Isaac's sleep-softened face. At the loss, he discovered a burst of energy he didn't expect and rolled to his side. Without a plan, his fingers found Isaac's hip beneath the covers. Daniel hoped the small connection would soothe the unnamed emotions scratching at his brain.

A faint hint of light peeked around the curtains. It was early. If he fell asleep right now, he might get a few hours in before Isaac woke. Daniel's brain wouldn't shut down. His fingers slid over Isaac's oblique. Isaac didn't stir. Daniel questioned if he hoped the man would wake. He flattened his palm against Isaac's abdomen, fighting the urge to keep touching him. It wasn't fair for him to always be so demanding of Isaac. Before he realized what he was doing, Daniel traced Isaac's navel. A deep rumble of laughter filled the space between them. Isaac rolled, pinning him to the bed with his massive weight.

"Go to sleep."

"I can't," Daniel admitted. "I want to do something. Let's do something."

"Like what?" Isaac asked, sounding more asleep than awake.

Daniel didn't even think about it before answering. "I have to go to Colorado next. Come with me. Let's run away for a few days."

"I have to help Aden with Remy's birthday party today." Isaac still didn't sound awake.

"Afterward."

"Have mercy on me and go to sleep, and I'll do whatever you want."

A smile pulled at Daniel's lips. "Okay." Daniel closed his eyes, determined to do just that. He made it less than five minutes. "You're like a very warm blanket." With a huff, Isaac tensed as if to move away. Daniel tightened his hold. "I didn't say I didn't like it."

"Are we sleeping here or..."

Daniel thought it over. "Am I invited to Remy's party?"

"I just invited you."

"Then I need to buy him a present."

"Well, now I'm awake," Isaac bitched, sounding like a kid.

Daniel couldn't stop smiling. "I think I can sleep now."

"Jesus Ch—" Isaac bit off. "You're killing me."

"You're very sexy for a dead man," Daniel said, hoping to make it better.

Isaac grunted. Daniel took it to mean he was mollified. He made it five more minutes. "Isaac, you asleep?"

Isaac jumped. "Not now."

"Thank you."

"For what?" Isaac asked, even as he pressed a light kiss to Daniel's chest.

"For showing up."

Isaac moved closer, tucking Daniel tighter against his side. "This is the only place I want to be."

On that note, Daniel's eyes finally grew heavy. He'd be okay. His bullshit hadn't scared Isaac away yet. There was still time for him to be better.

"I HAVE A SERIOUS QUESTION."

Daniel tore his gaze away from Aden and focused on Isaac at his question. "Shoot."

"Am I boring you?"

A deep line appeared between Daniel's eyes. It took every ounce of Isaac's control not to smile. "Where did that come from?"

"You haven't stopped staring at Aden since we got here."

As if shaking off a trance, Daniel shook head. "Sorry. I'm obsessing."

The wicked smile pulling at the corners of Isaac's mouth was out of his control. "I thought I was your current obsession." Without giving Daniel time to respond, Isaac sidled closer. He shoved his hands in his pockets, matching Daniel's pose, and stared at Aden. "Tell me what you're turning over in your head and I'll join you."

It was hard to keep his gaze trained on Aden when Isaac could feel Daniel's laughter. He loved the man's smile. Isaac wanted to revel in it, but he also craved Daniel's thoughts.

"He's not acting right," Daniel said, obviously deciding to humor Isaac.

"Probably because everyone's staring at his husband," Isaac said, pointing out the obvious.

Daniel shook his head. "No. If you marry someone as hot as Remy, you're used to everyone always looking at him. I can't explain it. He doesn't look happy or... I don't know. Something."

Isaac mused over Daniel's observation. He was right. Aden looked pissed. The man should be ecstatic. He'd gone above and beyond to make Remy's birthday a smashing success. Remy hadn't stopped smiling all day. Everything was perfect. Isaac straightened away from the short wall surrounding the pool. "Thinking situations over and coming up with the best possible scenario to fit the circumstances might be your thing, but being straightforward is mine. Let's go."

Daniel's eyes widened. "I'm sorry. What?"

With a nod in Aden's direction, Isaac repeated himself. "Come on." Without waiting to see if Daniel followed, Isaac headed for Aden. The red-haired giant was flipping burgers on the grill with more prejudice than Isaac had ever witnessed.

"Okay," Isaac said the moment he reached Aden's side. "What's wrong with you?"

Aden glanced up, looking resigned. He opened his mouth as if ready to spill. His eyes darted over Isaac's shoulder. "Oh, hey, Daniel."

Isaac glanced behind him before meeting Aden's gaze again. "Spill. You can trust Daniel. He might be a little bastard, but he's a good guy." Isaac didn't look to see Daniel's reaction. At the moment, Aden was the important one. His lips twisted into a small smile. It felt like a win. The smile fell as he glanced Remy's way, as if checking to make sure the man wasn't looking. Aden reached in his back pocket and handed Isaac a folded card.

"It's from Remy's mom. A delivery driver brought it along with some flowers earlier. I shouldn't have opened it, but I had a bad feeling."

Isaac opened the card and read aloud for Daniel's benefit. "Happy birthday, my gorgeous son. I got an invite from the beast, but I won't be attending. It's my hope you'll come see me when you have time, but as long as you're married to that man, I won't be coming to see you." Isaac folded the card and met Aden's gaze once more. Horror owned him. There was nothing he could say. Instinct took over. Without thought, he slipped the card between the grate on the grill. "Oops."

Aden didn't smile. "He'll still find out eventually."

"But she doesn't have to ruin his birthday," Isaac shot back.

"What's her phone number?"

Daniel's question had Isaac and Aden turning his way. Aden was the first to break. "Nu-uh. There's nothing to be done here but make things worse."

Daniel's jaw was set in a hard line. He dug his phone from his pocket. "You may as well give it to me, because you know I can get it without you."

Aden swiped his hand over his face, looking horrified yet resigned. He dug his phone out, found the number, and rattled it off.

Daniel's face was harder than Isaac had ever seen, but his tone didn't match as Remy's mother answered. "Mrs. Bergeau. This is Daniel Long with the *Daily Sports Report.* I'm here at your son's birthday party, waiting to take a photo for an article of him along with his husband and parents. Since you haven't arrived yet, and I have other engagements, I wondered when I could expect you?"

Isaac couldn't tear his gaze away from Daniel. This man was amazing.

Daniel listened for a moment before countering whatever she had to say. "Really? When I spoke with your son earlier, he assured me that you would be here. He said you'd never miss his birthday."

Isaac smiled.

Daniel winked. "My readers love a good story about happy families. Remy is a favorite. He hasn't stopped smiling since he married Aden. It's always our pleasure to feature them in our paper." He nodded at whatever she was saying. "Yes, ma'am. I know both Remy and Aden very well. They're the happiest couple I've ever seen. Hold on a sec," Daniel said, before snapping a pic of Remy on the sly. He pressed the phone to his ear once more. "I've just sent you a picture of the birthday boy. Yes, ma'am. He does look happy. Yes, ma'am. I'm also glad he's living an open life. What time can I expect you? Yes, I'll hold while you check flight times."

Isaac's cheeks ached from his huge smile. Damn, he wanted to kiss Daniel. Daniel smirked as he held Isaac's stare, as if he could read Isaac's mind.

"Yes, ma'am," Daniel said, going back to his call. "I think I'm good to hang out that long. Should I tell Remy your flight was delayed? No, ma'am. I'm not above lying to a friend if it's for a good cause. Seeing his mother on his birthday seems like a good cause to me." Daniel nodded again. "Yes, ma'am. If I see a flower delivery, I'll be sure to toss the card before anyone gets to it."

Isaac bit his bottom lip to keep from laughing.

"I will see you tonight. Have a good flight," Daniel said before ending the call. He focused on Aden. "There. No need to worry. She'll be here before nine."

Aden blinked, looking like he'd narrowly missed being sideswiped by a truck. "How did you do that?"

Daniel shrugged. "No one likes bad press."

"Thank you," Aden said, sounding like it physically hurt him to do so.

Daniel waved it off. "You'd better go tell Remy his mom's flight was delayed."

Aden nodded and started to walk away before backtracking. "By the way, I'm sorry about yesterday."

Isaac's eyebrows rose at the apology. Not only had he never heard Aden apologize to anyone, he was beyond curious what the man had done to be sorry about.

"Think nothing of it," Daniel said with a bland smile. "Water under the bridge."

Isaac wasn't sure Aden even made it out of earshot before he broke. "What the hell was that all about? What did Aden do?"

Daniel winked. "It's hardly water under the bridge if I repeat it, now is it? Anyhow, look how happy Remy is."

Without thought, Isaac turned his head. Daniel was right. Remy looked ready to jump up and down. He was all but levitating in his chair. "You're an amazing person," Isaac said without thought or looking Daniel's way.

Daniel touched his lips to Isaac's ear. "We have a long day ahead of us. We should find a spot to hide and make out."

"Do you think you could stop at just making out?" Isaac had to ask because he knew he couldn't.

"Let's find out." The growl in Daniel's voice had Isaac's feet moving. Even if they couldn't stop there, Isaac couldn't keep standing there. After all, it was only a matter of time before people noticed his erection.

7

The view from Daniel's hotel balcony of the Colorado mountains wasn't anywhere near as gorgeous as the man leaning against the railing and enjoying the skyline. With no real plan in mind, Daniel wrapped his arms around Isaac's waist and pulled the man against his chest. He nipped at Isaac's nape.

"It's beautiful here," Isaac said, sounding breathless.

"You're beautiful," Daniel countered as he kissed the side of Isaac's neck.

Isaac's deep breathing was the only indication he gave that Daniel's manhandling was getting to him. "Can you believe I've never been here before?"

"The mountains in Tennessee are beautiful too, especially this time of year. Have you ever been there?" Daniel asked as he kept up the torture, going as far as to grind against Isaac's ass.

"No."

In Daniel's head, he was smiling like an evil bastard at the desperation of Isaac's single word. He couldn't resist sliding his hands down Isaac's body and cupping his erection through his jeans. "You should go with me the next time I make the trip."

"Just let me know when." Isaac dropped his chin to his chest, giving Daniel better access to his nape.

"I love how easily you agree to keep seeing me."

Isaac shifted slightly in Daniel's hold, capturing Daniel's lips over his shoulder. Their tongues entwined momentarily before Daniel went back to biting the side of Isaac's neck. "This is no hardship," Isaac said, reaching behind him and kneading Daniel's aching cock through his pants.

Daniel spun Isaac in his arms. "No one can see us," he swore as he slid Isaac's zipper down. Each balcony of the posh hotel was private and facing the mountainside. There was no way anyone would spot them, but the idea of having Isaac out in the open was tantalizing. With the front of Isaac's jeans spread wide, Daniel shoved his hand inside and palmed Isaac's hard dick. His mouth watered. "God-damn, Isaac. You're always ready for me." Pre-cum smeared across his palm. Daniel licked it away before going back for more. The sound of Isaac panting was the only sound filling Daniel's ears. "I want to eat that ass," Daniel growled, spinning Isaac once more before peeling the man's jeans down his hips. Once he had Isaac nude from the waist down, Daniel used Isaac's pants to keep from tearing up his knees when he knelt between Isaac's spread legs and dove in. Isaac held on to the railing. His panting turned to moans as Daniel tongued his asshole and tugged on the man's dick. They were so amazing together. Daniel had never been higher than he'd been since meeting Isaac. He never had to sweet talk Isaac into doing anything. Daniel simply bent the man over and did as he pleased.

Right now, he wanted to tear up this ass. Daniel wanted to lick it and toy with it before burying himself inside. The way Isaac's ass always sucked him deeper was addictive. Daniel was mindless to everything. There was no art or skill to his playing. He simply touched Isaac everywhere while fantasizing about fucking him. Hot cum coated his hand as Isaac muffled his cries. Still, Daniel couldn't stop. He kept pumping Isaac's cock as if it was his. Even as he kissed his way up Daniel's spine and probed the man's asshole with his dick, Daniel didn't stop. The sounds coming from Isaac drove him on almost as much as his own need. Isaac was a power trip.

His crown jumped for joy as it pushed past the tight ring of muscles. Isaac's body took over, pulling him deeper inside. A low hiss escaped Daniel. Isaac was so goddamn tight. When he clamped down on Daniel, the way he did now, Daniel always worried he'd end up permanently damaged.

"Oh, shit. Right there, Daniel. Jesus. I'm gonna come again."

That was all the warning Daniel got before Isaac's body tightened and convulsed around his cock. The move milked out Daniel's orgasm before he was ready. Squeezing his eyes closed, Daniel gasped his way through the waves of pleasure. His hips rotated, still trying to get even deeper. The tips of his fingers went numb as they dug into Isaac's sides, holding him in place as his hips slammed against the man's ass. His head was empty. Isaac always took him to a place where nothing existed but the two of them. Aftershocks made his dick twitch. Daniel tried steadying his breathing. His heart tried beating its way from his chest.

"Goddamn, Isaac. Goddamn," he gasped, incapable of finding the words for what it was like for him being with Isaac.

HIS DAY STARTED with sitting on the sidelines as Daniel interviewed an ex-champion snowboarder who recently started a charity to help underprivileged children learn the sport. Now, as the sun dipped low, Isaac sat wrapped in nothing more than a blanket while holding Daniel. They'd been staring at the view from a chaise lounge for over an hour. Tomorrow, he'd return to his real life, training for his next match. Daniel would head out to wherever he was off to next. Each time they parted ways, Isaac expected it would be the final time.

"How do you feel about me stopping by when I can?" Daniel's question proved how connected they were.

Isaac tried playing it cool. His smile wouldn't abate. "I'd like that. Maybe I can meet you when I'm traveling for fights too?"

Daniel kissed his neck. "Don't worry over that, babe. You're already overwhelmed. I'll come to you."

"I'm trying to look after you. I get the impression no one else does."

He felt Daniel shrug against his chest. "You're taking care of me right now. I'm pretty low maintenance."

Against his better judgment, a chuckle escaped Isaac. "My sore muscles beg to differ. Not that I'm complaining," Isaac tacked on before Daniel got the wrong impression.

"That's your fault," Daniel said, not sounding the least bit apologetic. "You shouldn't be so sexy."

Isaac toyed with Daniel's fingers. No matter how hard he tried, he couldn't stop touching the man. "Guess I'd better stay in shape, then. I'd hate for you to stop coming around."

Daniel twisted and met Isaac's stare. "I didn't mean your

looks. You're sexy. That has nothing to do with your appearance."

Isaac didn't know what to say. That was the hottest thing anyone had ever said to him.

Daniel smirked. "Not that I'm complaining about your looks."

For the first time in his life, Isaac wanted more. He wanted to keep this man. A deep craving rose in his gut, making him long to know everything about Daniel from his shoe size to what age he started walking. "Do your parents call you Daniel? Or are you Danny to your family?"

Daniel's smirk fell, and he settled back down into Isaac's arms. "I don't have a family. They signed me over to the state when I was twelve after I landed in Juvy for the third time." Daniel snorted. "Some people are born bad, so they cut their losses."

Outrage owned Isaac. For real, he had a special hatred for people who gave up on their kids. "You're an amazing person, so it's their loss. I think I'll keep calling you Daniel."

"That's a good thing, since it's my name."

Even though Daniel didn't sound upset after confessing his parents were scum, Isaac couldn't fight the urge to make him happy. "After screaming it more than a few times, I'm attached to it. But I could come up with a pet name too. How do you feel about Sir Snuggles?"

Daniel was staring at him again. The horror written in the man's every line was priceless. "I'm not above stabbing you in your sleep."

Isaac chewed his bottom lip, trying hard not to laugh. "I'll come up with something." The way Daniel grunted could've meant anything at all. Since Daniel didn't seem thrilled at the idea of having a pet name, Isaac chose a different topic. "Do you mind if I ask you something?"

"You're always free to ask whatever you want. I love a curious mind."

Isaac smiled at the honesty in Daniel's voice. "What made you invite me back to your hotel room that first time?"

"Eye contact," Daniel said without missing a beat.

A bark of laughter escaped Isaac before he could call it back. "What's that supposed to mean?"

Daniel stroked Isaac's chest. The unexpected loving gesture had Isaac's heartbeat kicking up a notch. "There's only two reasons a man makes eye contact with another man as intensely as you were trying to do with me. One is during a job interview, because you're thinking about it. Two, if you're intent on rocking their world. No matter what I did—I played on my phone and everything—you didn't give up trying to hold my stare." He felt Daniel's lips shape into a smile against his chest, and Isaac hated the loss of seeing the man's sexy smirk. "I tested you with that cellphone bit. When you didn't give up, I knew you'd be perfect for me. I was right."

Daniel always took the strangest roads to get to the point, but then the most awesome shit came out of the man's mouth. Everyone else paled by comparison. Isaac had never been more scared of anyone in his life. It was terrifying to know he'd never meet another man who held a candle to Daniel, and he didn't doubt for a second they were temporary.

July

Isaac: *Aden is having a Fourth of July BBQ. Want to come?*
Daniel: *Yes, I'd love to come.*
Isaac: *I read that as sexual.*

Daniel: *I meant it that way.*
Isaac: *Phone sex?*
Daniel: *Calling now.*

Isaac: *So... next weekend?*
Daniel: *How about tomorrow?*
Isaac: *Yes, please?*

August

Daniel: *Why is it so damn hot here?*
Isaac: *I don't know where you are, but it's summer.*
Daniel: *Open your door.*

Isaac: *You say you're not one to sneak away but you're gone.*
Daniel: *Just clearing some things away so I can come back tomorrow.*
Isaac: *I'll accept this excuse.*
Daniel: *Sexy and magnanimous. I knew I kept coming back for a reason.*
Isaac: *Yeah, that's why.*

Daniel: *How did your latest fight go?*
Isaac: *I won.*
Daniel: *You have no idea how much I hate having missed it.*
Isaac: *You can't be everywhere at once.*

Daniel: *I can try.*

Daniel: *If I took a week off work, would you spend it with me?*

Isaac: *I would love that.*

Daniel: *Good, because I'm in the parking lot with a week's worth of luggage.*

ISAAC: *What would it take to make you turn around and come back? I need you inside me.*

Daniel: *A base salary of $350K and unlimited travel funds. I have to work, but I'll find a way. Being inside you is worth more than all the money in the world.*

Isaac: *Go make money. I just had a moment of weakness. Sorry.*

Daniel: *Never apologize for wanting me.*

Isaac: *That wasn't an apology for wanting you. That was me being sorry for being needy. I'm proud of you. I love knowing you're doing your thing.*

Daniel: *Blanket rule—no apologies from you.*

8

*O*ctober

Daniel: *Do you remember my offer to take you to the TN mountains?*

Isaac: *I do.*

Daniel: *I'm headed there today. Would you like to join me?*

Isaac: *Damn. I have family in town. Plus, Remy and Aden are in NOLA. As soon as my family leaves, I have to open every day for the rest of the week.*

Daniel: *Damn. Guess I'll have to jack off on the balcony in memory of our time enjoying the sights together.*

Isaac: *Pics or it didn't happen.*

Daniel: *LOL! I miss you.*

Isaac: *I miss you too.*

Isaac: *P.S. Why are you headed to Tennessee on such short notice? I thought you were typing articles all day.*

Daniel: *I did some volunteer work there a few months back. Now this company wants to give me a plaque.*

Isaac: *You're a good person.*

He wasn't a good person, but Isaac believed it. That was

why he was driving straight from Tennessee to Key Largo. No one would ever understand how intoxicating it was for him to have Isaac believing in him. There'd been less than a handful of people who'd thought he was worth the air he took up his entire life.

According to Isaac's text, he had family in town. But that had been two days ago. Surely they'd be gone by now. He hoped so. It wasn't that Daniel didn't want to meet Isaac's family. He just wasn't ready. Not to mention, he treasured the time they spent alone, and Daniel didn't have much. This trip would be short. He managed to squeeze Isaac between Tennessee and Alabama trips. Daniel hoped to make the most of every second together. His mood was shit for no reason other than it was shit, which was usually the case. He wanted it to end. Isaac always chased the darkness away.

The gym's parking lot was full, forcing Daniel to take the only open parking space, directly in front of the door. He hated that shit. People around here were all chatty as hell. He didn't want to talk. Rather than risking being stopped, Daniel left his bags in the car. He could get them later after the gym closed. For now, he used the extra time to make it up the back stairs before anyone could pop from the front and stop him. When he reached the top, Daniel stared at the wooden slab, separating him from Isaac. He took a deep breath, calming his impatience. Each mile he'd gotten closer to Isaac, the more Daniel's hunger rose. In a matter of seconds, he'd get to kiss the lips he'd been longing for. There was nothing better.

A SERIES of knocks landed on the front door, forcing Isaac to drop Trina's luggage in kitchen. These fucking gym guys. For real, they never gave him a moment's peace. He'd told them he was busy with family and to call Gunnar if they had any problems. With Aden and Remy in New Orleans, they seemed twice as needy, but—so far—they'd honored his wishes and left him in peace. Apparently, that was at an end.

"Are you expecting someone?"

With a shrug, Isaac headed for the door. "It's probably just one of the guys from the gym."

"Mmmm, gym guys."

"No," Isaac growled over his shoulder.

Trina was smiling. As usual, he couldn't tell if she was joking or if he'd have to kill someone. Giving up on the topic for now, he threw open the door. Daniel stood on the other side. Without thought, Isaac's gaze dropped to the man's toes. He slowly inspected every inch. Light-colored shorts against tan legs. A pale-yellow shirt that made the man's eyes seem softer. Goddamn. Isaac was a lucky bastard. Still, this was a surprise and not a good time. "You're here."

A sexy-sounding chuckle fell from gorgeous lips. "Yeah. Don't trip over yourself to let me in, or is this a bad time?"

"Invite your friend in."

Isaac winced as Trina's words floated through the air. Daniel's eyebrows rose. It was too late. After taking a step back, Isaac waved Daniel inside. "Come in."

Before Isaac could think of what to say, Trina stepped forward, holding her hand out for Daniel to shake. "Hi. I'm Trina."

"Daniel," Daniel said, shaking her hand and looking beyond confused.

"I figured as much. Dad talks about you all the time."

Somehow, Daniel's eyebrows managed to go higher. "Dad? But you're grown... and white."

Trina's snort said a thousand things. Mostly, that she was enjoying herself a bit too much. Isaac bit his bottom lip to keep from laughing.

"So are you. Yet, here we both are." Without waiting for Daniel's response, Trina turned on Isaac. "I'm sorry this was such a short visit, but I have to get to the airport, and you know how Miami traffic can be."

He hugged her, trying not to let Daniel's presence steal a precious moment from him. Daniel would either deal with this or he wouldn't. It was out of Isaac's control. "Are you sure you don't want me to go with you?"

She squeezed him harder. "Don't be ridiculous. I have a rental to return. How would you get back home?"

She had a point. He could feel Daniel's stare boring a hole in his skin. "At least let me walk you to your car."

She pulled away, smiling. He'd never been prouder of anyone in his life. "That, you can do. I don't want to carry these suitcases."

Against his will, a snort escaped Isaac. "I should've known it was a setup." He focused on Daniel. The man was still eyeing them with a deep line between his brows. "Give me a minute to walk her out, and we'll talk." Daniel gave a sharp nod. He didn't look happy. Isaac couldn't help that.

"I won't keep him long," Trina promised. "It was nice meeting you, Daniel."

"You too," Daniel said, sounding so genuine it gave Isaac pause. Their gazes locked as Isaac passed Daniel with Trina's suitcases in hand. Before Isaac knew it would happen, their lips brushed too. Daniel's timing was bad, but Isaac couldn't deny he'd missed the man. He would hurry back, even if Daniel was pissed over this secret. That kiss wasn't near enough.

Isaac should've known Trina wouldn't let the moment pass without comment. They didn't even make it down the stairs. Hell, they barely made it out of earshot. "So you didn't tell your man about me? Why is that?"

"I wasn't hiding you."

Trina glanced over her shoulder and winked. "I know you'd never do that. So, why?"

They made it to Trina's rental car before Isaac found an answer. "I don't know if he's serious about me, I guess?" He shrugged, feeling uncomfortable. "It sounds stupid, I know, but I didn't want to give him too much of myself if he doesn't want it."

Trina nodded. "That makes sense." A bright smile exploded across her face. "But kudos to you. He's gorgeous. Like a nerdy bad boy."

Isaac rolled his eyes and pulled her in for another hug. "You'd better get gone before your flight leaves without you."

She held on tight. "I love the new place." She pulled away and met his gaze. "And you."

"I love you too."

"You be good," Trina said sternly as if she was the parent.

He scoffed. "As if."

She rolled her eyes at his mock teenager voice. "I'm the one who's supposed to cause trouble. Be the adult."

He stamped his foot. "Damn it. If I gotta."

"Yes, you gotta. I love you."

His smile grew by the second. "I love you too. Call me when you land."

Trina climbed inside her car. "I will."

With a final kiss on her cheek, Isaac closed her door and shoved her suitcases in the trunk. She waved and was gone, leaving him with no other choice but to face Daniel.

He hadn't thought this would become an issue. Daniel didn't seem like the type man who came back for more. Isaac wanted more. That thought kept his feet moving back to where he'd left Daniel. He found Daniel sitting in his favorite recliner, staring at nothing. Isaac closed the door with more of a snap than necessary. Daniel's gaze jumped to his. Damn, the man was so sexy.

"You have a daughter."

It seemed there'd be no niceties. "Yes. I told you I had family in town."

Daniel pursed his lips as if trying to decide where to start asking questions. Isaac didn't see a need to make the man dig for answers. He moved across the room and dropped onto the couch. "Years ago, I was fighting for a small gym in Vegas. There wasn't a single big-name fighter in the bunch, but you know fighters. We're a tight-knit bunch." Daniel nodded and Isaac kept talking. "One day, our trainer, Dave, came in and said one of our own needed some help. He said there was a fighter who was married to a pediatric nurse, and one of her favorite patients was in dire need of a bone marrow transplant. She was running out of time." Isaac shrugged, remembering those days and how blasé he'd been about the entire ordeal. "I thought, what the hell. If I could help out a fellow fighter and a kid, I'd give it a shot. So, I went down and got tested, thinking it would never go further."

Isaac shook his head. A self-deprecating smile tugged at his lips. Daniel kept watching him, as if hanging on every word and waiting for the point, so Isaac kept trying to give it to him.

"I was a match. Turned out, the fighter whose wife worked at the hospital was Drew Alexander. For someone like me, a nobody, finding myself the center of the world heavyweight champion's attention was surreal as fuck. Even crazier than that was meeting the extraordinary little girl who needed my help."

"Trina?" Daniel asked, obviously hearing the love in Isaac's voice.

Isaac nodded. "Her family had buckled under the strain of the cost of keeping her alive and given her up to the state years earlier. The hospital was the only home she knew. I hadn't spent much time around kids, but she was like an adult trapped in a dying child's body." Isaac shrugged. "I can't explain it. I just fell in love. Drew, being the amazing guy he is, agreed to pay her medical bills and all the adoption fees. He also offered to train me. The adoption didn't go through until after Trina turned eighteen, but she's still my daughter." Daniel didn't say a word. It was unnerving. Isaac kept rambling, filling the uncomfortable silence. "She's pretty amazing. Smart as hell. She's a freshman at UCLA." Still, Daniel silently waited, as if expecting a catch or something more. Isaac brushed his palms on his shorts. "Feel free to jump in at any moment."

Daniel's mouth lifted in one corner. "There's so much more to you than meets the eye." Isaac didn't know how to respond, especially considering the way Daniel stared at him. He couldn't get a good read on Daniel's mood, but the way the man looked at Isaac had his mouth watering. "Still," Daniel tacked on, sounding regretful. "We've been seeing each other for four months now and you never mentioned a daughter. Surely that deserves some punishment."

Isaac ignored the images Daniel's threat brought to mind. Instead, he focused on the first half of Daniel's claim.

"You never said we were exclusive. Trina may be grown, but I'm still not parading her out for every man I meet."

Something dangerous flashed in Daniel's eyes. "Are you saying you've been seeing other people between our visits?"

"I'm saying I didn't want to assume you weren't."

Daniel eyes narrowed and Isaac knew he'd fucked up. "Do I strike you as the type of man who would show up here at least once a week, traveling thousands of miles to see you, on a whim?"

Damn, he really didn't want Isaac to answer that. Daniel was the type man who could do as he pleased. It wasn't a stretch to think he'd fill his time, using Isaac's body if he was bored that day. Isaac scrambled for something to say. "I haven't wanted anyone else since meeting you."

"You didn't answer my question."

Isaac tried his damnedest to avoid doing so. "I think you could have anyone." He thought it over before adding, "But, I also think, if I truly believed for a second you were with someone else, I'd kill them." As he made the admission, Isaac realized how much he meant the words.

THE INTENSITY in Isaac's voice and stare wiped Daniel clean. For the first time in Daniel's life, he didn't feel like he was too much for someone. All the obsessing he'd done, wondering if he was showing too much interest, coming around too often, or demanding too much from Isaac sexually vanished underneath the passion in Isaac's tone.

"My bag is in the car. Am I staying?"

Isaac's intensity didn't ebb. "Try to leave. I dare you."

Daniel went hard at the threat. They were a dangerous combination always on the verge of exploding. "We should skip to the part where I dominate you until you beg for mercy."

For a moment, Isaac didn't respond. His shoulders expanded as he took a deep breath. "Goddamn," he finally groaned, making Daniel's dick leak.

"I want you in the bedroom and nude before I count to ten."

Isaac stood, unquestioning. A knock sounded through the apartment. Isaac growled. "I can see why Aden didn't stay in this apartment long before buying his house. People never stop knocking on the damn door." He headed in that direction.

Daniel came to his feet. "I believe I told you to take your clothes off."

Isaac eyed the door.

Daniel's eyebrows hit his hairline. Isaac had never disobeyed him before. He wouldn't start today. "Bedroom. Now." Without looking back, Isaac headed for the bedroom. Daniel went for the door. He opened it, finding Mateo on the other side. "No."

He didn't wait for Mateo to speak before slamming the door closed again. Another knock sounded. Daniel took a deep breath before answering. He felt his features harden as he transformed into the harsh taskmaster only Isaac got to see. He met Mateo's stare. "I said no. Isaac is busy. I'm busy. He isn't here to see to your every need or hold your hand through every chore. Whatever it is, it can wait until he's back on the clock." On that note, Daniel slammed the door again, locking it for good measure. This time, no sound came from the other side. It wouldn't have mattered to him if Mateo had kept at it. Daniel had plans. If he lived here, no one would ever take advantage of Isaac, and Isaac obviously needed a keeper. No one demanded anything from the man but Daniel.

When he reached the bedroom, Daniel's footsteps slowed. Isaac stood nude in the center room, his hard cock waiting for Daniel. As always when he was with Isaac, some form of fucked-up mixture of impatience and a need to drag things out rose in Daniel. The desire to bury his dick in that sexy ass made Daniel physically ache. His mind needed something more. He craved seeing how far Isaac would go for him.

Without asking permission, Daniel headed for Isaac's bedside table. He'd been there enough times to get lube and condoms that he knew Isaac wouldn't question the intrusion. However, that wasn't Daniel's only goal today. Those weren't the only items Isaac kept inside. Daniel pulled out a ten-inch dildo with a suction cup at the end. Without glancing Isaac's way, he coated the lifelike toy with lube before moving to the wooden bench at the foot of the bed. He secured it to the bench.

Daniel finally met Isaac's stare. "Sit."

Isaac's mouth lifted in one corner, tightening the muscles in Daniel's stomach. Without a word of argument, Isaac moved to the bench, positioned the dildo at his asshole, and sat. The man's nostrils flared in the sexiest way as he took the whole toy inside. The front of Daniel's underwear was soaked. Daniel held Isaac's gaze and stripped. Once he was nude, Daniel retrieved the bottle of lube and moved the chair from Isaac's desk to where he could sit across from Isaac. He sat.

"Fuck your toy."

While using the edge of the bench for leverage, Isaac eased up until the toy was only inserted close to an inch before dropping down again. He set a pattern, riding the huge dildo while holding Daniel's gaze. For a minute, Daniel watched the show, letting the lust build and torment him. Lately, it seemed as if Isaac was the only thing keeping him from rocking himself in the corner—moments like these with the man. It was Daniel's biggest fear Isaac would see him for the nut job he really was and leave him in the dust. That time hadn't come yet.

Daniel popped the top on the lube and squirted a generous amount in his hand. He fisted Isaac's cock, pumping as Isaac rode the fake dick. Isaac's eyes were unfocused. His lips were swollen from chewing on them. He was the picture of sexiness on the verge of orgasm.

Daniel squeezed, twisted, and tugged. Isaac moaned like a tortured soul. A smile that felt evil, even to him, tugged at Daniel's lips. Sweat glistened on Isaac's skin. "Is there anything you wouldn't do for me?" Daniel asked as the darkness inside him unexpectedly rose.

"No," Isaac gasped, sounding desperate.

"What if I told you to stop and left you hanging right here?"

A whimper fell from Isaac's sexy lips, but he didn't back down. "I'd stop."

Daniel continued stroking the silky skin in his hand, not making good on his threat. "What if I told you to come?"

A cry tore from Isaac's throat, filling the room as hot cum coated Daniel's hand and hit his thighs. Daniel didn't stop tugging. He needed every wave of ecstasy. He also didn't stop watching Isaac's every reaction. The man always owned his orgasms. He moaned and panted—teeth bared.

The urge to fist his own cock was immense—almost matching his need to kiss Isaac. Daniel did neither. He held tight to his control, strengthening his will.

"Suck me."

At his demand, Isaac let the toy fall from his ass before dropping to his knees between Daniel's. Daniel clung to the arms of the chair as Isaac lowered his head and swallowed Daniel's dick. Against his will, Daniel's eyes fell closed. Isaac wasn't playing around. The hot suction on his cock was intense. The noises Isaac made around Daniel's erection screamed how much the man loved sucking dick. It was a huge turn-on. Even though Daniel wanted to lift his hips and fuck the man's throat until he gagged, Daniel held still. Every muscle in his body was hard enough to snap a tendon. He ground his back teeth, fighting back his orgasm. Dropping his chin to his chest, Daniel watched Isaac's head bob up and down in his lap. The bottom of Daniel's feet dug into the floor as he braced himself. His knees ached from the pressure. Saliva dripped from his balls onto the chair, pooling between his legs. Daniel savored every sensation. Isaac hummed. Daniel exploded. His dick pulsed and tiny sparks ran up his length. Gasps tore from his throat as Isaac continued sucking as if Daniel's cum was his favorite meal. When the insanity passed, Isaac still didn't move from his spot on the floor. Instead, he placed light kisses on Daniel's half hard cock. After he'd kissed every inch, he moved to Daniel's lower abs, kissing his way up Daniel's body. Daniel held the man's head to his body, scared as hell of losing the connection.

He felt too much. This wasn't supposed to happen. Isaac would leave one day. Everyone always did. All Daniel had was himself and this moment. He didn't want it to end. By the time their mouths clashed, Daniel was borderline insane with the need to cling to Isaac for as long as possible. He sucked on the man's tongue and scratched at his skin. If he'd ever been more desperate, Daniel couldn't remember it.

"I want you here," Isaac said between kisses, as if the desperation was his. "For as long as you're willing," he added, further proving how their thoughts matched in intensity. Daniel couldn't know what would happen with them. All he knew was—he'd met someone he couldn't function without, and he'd never been more terrified.

9

*D*aniel had come to town with the new arrivals from No Rival. Isaac's eyeballs itched with the need to watch him. Rather than taking his mock interview to lunch, as he'd done in the past, Daniel took today's interview into Aden's office. Isaac wasn't getting any work done. He tried. In fact, he'd sparred with Carter—one of Drew Alexander's star MMA fighters who was back for his second round of Aden's training. Isaac's head wasn't in it. It was in Aden's office, licking Daniel.

By the time the office door opened and Daniel stepped out, Isaac was damn near dancing in place. Mateo kept eyeballing him. Isaac kept ignoring him. Still, Isaac fucking hated that he was on the clock. He wanted to cross the room, meet Daniel halfway, and capture the man's lips. It had been four fucking days since he'd gotten a taste. It was hell.

As he looked on, Daniel shook hands with the man he'd been interviewing before parting ways. His gaze locked on Isaac. Isaac's blood pounded in his ears. The rest of the gym disappeared. There was a connection between them. Isaac knew in his gut Daniel felt the same longing to see him.

"Hey."

Isaac's knees weakened at the sexy way Daniel said that single word. "Hey, I—"

"I feel like I've seen you a lot the last few months," Mateo said, sidling in between them and interrupting Isaac.

Isaac's gaze shot to Daniel. He couldn't miss Daniel's reaction to Mateo's observation. Isaac wasn't disappointed. A slow and wicked smile spread across Daniel's lips. "I'm finding Key Largo fascinating. Something new catches my eye each time I visit." His gaze flickered in Isaac's direction as he made the claim. "I can't stay away."

Mateo's expression turned calculating. "Have you been to Slip since Boston and Kaz built the dance floor and bar on the veranda?"

"Strangely, I have not. I usually keep better track of such big fish, but I've been keeping busy."

"A bunch of us are headed up there tonight. You should come with us."

Daniel glanced Isaac's way. "What do you think? Should we go?"

The smile pulling at Isaac's lips was out of his control. Daniel obviously wanted to be here and didn't care if anyone knew they were together. Isaac didn't care where they went. He was just damn grateful for having met this awesome man. "Sounds like fun. I'll have to meet you there, though, since I don't get off until nine."

"I can wait for you," Daniel offered.

Isaac shook his head. "Don't worry over it. Go. Have a few drinks." His mouth lifted in one corner, matching the smirk in Isaac's heart as he added, "Loosen up."

"What about you?" Mateo asked a passing Remy, seeming oblivious to the heat flaring between Isaac and Daniel.

Remy froze. His gaze darted from one person to the next. He tugged on the neck of his red tank top, looking ready to bolt. "What about me?"

"You going to Slip with us tonight?"

Remy pulled a face. "No, thank you."

Isaac didn't know why, but he always got the impression Remy didn't like Boston. He could understand Boston choosing not to work out in the same gym where Gunnar worked. Everyone knew they used to date, but Remy liked everyone. For some reason, Boston was the exception.

Mateo tried maneuvering Remy away from the group. He lowered his voice, but not enough. "We could go somewhere else."

Aden appeared out of nowhere, carrying a set of weights back to where they belonged. He walked between Remy and Mateo.

"Make better life choices before I'm forced to kill you," Aden said without slowing.

Mateo took a step back. "You got it," he said, going back to his workout.

Isaac shook his head. The man was a huge mess. Giving up on him, Isaac glanced Daniel's way. He was watching Isaac as if he'd been waiting for Isaac to notice. "So, Slip around ten?"

Daniel nodded. "I have some business to take care of before then." There was a hint of heat in Daniel's gaze, but there was something else, as well. Isaac wished he knew what it was. "Don't make me wait too long tonight," Daniel said before pulling his keys from his front pocket. "I'd better get going or you'll never get anything done."

Isaac nodded. His lips tingled with the need to kiss Daniel. He hated that the man was leaving, and he had to act like it meant nothing.

"You should walk me out," Daniel suggested, as if his thoughts matched Isaac's.

Without a word, Isaac headed for the front door. He didn't look to see if anyone watched them go. All Isaac needed was one taste of Daniel's lips to tide him over until tonight.

———

IT FELT like an eternity before Isaac made it to Slip. He'd been forced to ruthlessly guard the chair next to him to keep Mateo from stealing Isaac's seat. They'd spent some time at the bar and had only managed to snag a table ten minutes before Isaac finally came through the door. His black t-shirt molded to his skin, straining against Isaac's biceps. Daniel took a breath, trying to push down the darkness inside him. He knew—occasionally—he needed to share Isaac with the world. That didn't mean he had to like it.

Five minutes after Isaac claimed the seat at his side, the man's hand slid up the inside of Daniel's thigh. Daniel kept his gaze locked straight ahead, hoping no one noticed the sweat forming on his skin. Carter was busy staring at the drink menu. Mateo was looking in every direction as if hunting a target. It was borderline maddening always wanting Isaac. It seemed the thrill should've faded at least a little. His interest hadn't waned a hair. A man wearing a Slip T-shirt, jeans, and an apron around his waist headed toward them.

"What can I get you?"

Mateo turned sideways in his chair as the waiter appeared over his shoulder, setting napkins on the table. His on-the-make smirk made an appearance. "If I could get your phone number, I won't ask for more, and promise to leave a huge tip."

Daniel worried he'd damage his eyes by not rolling them. To his surprise, the server turned a bright smile Mateo's way, obviously interested. It seemed the man got takers on occasion.

Before the man had time to respond, Carter butted in. "Don't mind him. He'll fuck anything that moves. It's not personal." Carter's speech was delivered without once looking the server's way. That was why he missed the flash of hurt passing over the man's features. The man walked away and moved to wait on the next table without a backward glance. The silence at the table was deafening. It took Carter a minute to finally look up from the drink menu. Daniel didn't know how the man hadn't felt all the eyes trained upon him. He glanced around. "What?"

Mateo looked thunderous. It was the first time Daniel had seen the man show any emotion he'd deem real. "You're an ass."

Carter shrugged. "Sorry, dude. I wasn't trying to cock block."

His apology only seemed to deepen Mateo's anger. "You're also dumb as fuck," Mateo added, not backing down. "You hurt that guy's feelings."

A hint of puzzled humor touched Carter's features. "Nowhere near as bad as you using him for the night and then forgetting his name would hurt."

Mateo shook his head. For a second, Daniel got a peek at the man behind the mask. He looked disappointed. "You know, not everyone is looking for a lifetime commitment. Some people are just trying to get through another shitty day alive, and you never know what other people are dealing with. Maybe you should consider that the next time you open your dumbass mouth and say some shit you can't take back." Without a backward glance, Mateo stood and went after the waiter Carter insulted.

"Well, on that note, I need another drink," Carter said, pushing from the table as well. "I'm going back to the bar."

Daniel didn't bother responding. He couldn't tear his gaze from Mateo and the server. The man was smiling again. Mateo was too. Their animated discussion kept Daniel enthralled. As he looked on, Mateo pushed the man's hair behind his ear. Even from where Daniel sat, he could see the man's blush. It was odd. The man was nice looking—tall and dark-haired, but Daniel didn't think Mateo had as much as looked at the man before asking for his number. It wasn't unusual for Daniel to obsess over things. He loved a good story and a mystery. Mateo was both.

"You know, it's customary to stare at your date and not other men when you're out with someone. Unless you'd rather stare at Mateo all night."

Daniel's head whipped around and his gaze snapped to Isaac's at the man's claim. "Sorry. I'm normally a damn good judge of character and I can't figure that one out. It's making me a bit insane."

A loud laugh came from Mateo's direction. Against his will, Daniel's gaze sought the pair once more. The server had his head thrown back on a roar of laughter. Mateo's smile looked genuine for once.

"I think I'll find a drink and someone to dance with," Isaac said, coming to his feet and snagging Daniel's attention once more.

"Damn it. I'm sorry. Let's dance," Daniel said, standing as well. Isaac's smile let him know he wasn't really annoyed. Daniel set his hand on the small of Isaac's back and steered him toward the veranda. The moment their skin met, Mateo was forgotten. This sexy man was the only person who needed his attention. He'd get it.

When they stepped outside into the warm night air, a love song filled the air. Several couples danced close under the tiny soft lights strung from the ceiling. The instant they reached the edge of the dance floor, Daniel pulled Isaac into his arms. Isaac didn't hesitate to close every inch between them, going flush against him. His hot breath brushed the side of Daniel's neck. Daniel's eyes fell closed as he savored the sensation. His feet automatically kept time with the music.

"Mateo isn't as complicated as you're making him out to be," Isaac said against the shell of Daniel's ear. The move had chill bumps rising on his skin. "He's unhappy to the point that he can't stand to see other people sad, so he fakes a bunch of smiles, trying to make other people smile. Part of him thinks if he fakes it enough, it'll eventually be true or if he gives enough happiness to others, it'll bring him joy. He's just trying to survive a hellish life."

He understood all too well the life Isaac described. Maybe that was why he couldn't stop obsessing over Mateo's personality. They were too much alike. Instead of admitting as much, he chose to make light of the conversation. "I thought you said it wasn't complicated."

A low chuckle caressed his ear and Isaac's body vibrated from the laughter. Daniel's chest tightened. He had to concentrate on something else. He liked Isaac. The last thing Daniel wanted was to destroy the man by falling for him. "It's the story I can't stop digging for," Daniel admitted. "That's who I am. I have to know why people do what they do. If he's trying to survive a hellish life, why is it hellish?"

He felt more than saw Isaac shrug. "Who knows? Everyone has a past and secrets."

"I want to know yours," Daniel said before he knew he would.

Isaac leaned away and met Daniel's stare. Taking Isaac's hand, Daniel headed for a nearby set of stairs, leading toward the beach. He didn't stop moving until they were at the water's edge. He needed a moment. The breeze coming off the ocean brushed over Daniel's skin. Daniel closed his eyes and breathed in the scent of salt and seaweed.

"This place really is beautiful." Daniel opened his eyes to find Isaac standing inches from him, staring him down. He'd seen the man at the height of intensity and at the edge of orgasm. Daniel had never seen the man wear the expression he did now. Isaac looked as if he braced himself for any reaction from Daniel. He wasn't wrong. Even Daniel didn't know what would happen next.

"I love you."

Daniel's mind blanked at Isaac's claim. "What?"

Isaac didn't back down. "You said you wanted my secrets. That's the only one I have left. Every time you leave here, it gets a little harder. I won't stop enduring it, because we both have careers we love, but I'm also in love with you. You might not want it, but it's there." For a moment, they simply held each other's stare. Isaac didn't look as if he waited to hear his words returned, but the pressure was real, nonetheless. The silence stretched on. A smile exploded across Isaac's face. "It's okay if you don't feel the same. That wasn't a—"

Daniel fisted the front of Isaac's shirt and hauled him forward. He held Isaac's stare. "No," he said, cutting off whatever Isaac had been about to say. Sometimes there were no words. This was one of those times. Isaac couldn't love him. Daniel didn't even love himself. No one should. "No," he repeated, releasing Isaac and taking a step back. Isaac's smile had fallen. His features were shut. Daniel couldn't know the man's thoughts, but he was certain they weren't good.

Isaac opened his mouth.

Whatever he'd been about to say, Daniel couldn't hear it. He held his hand up, stopping him. "Just no. Okay?"

"I'm sorry," Isaac said, making Daniel wonder if he'd stroke out.

"Are you fucking kidding me? Goddamn." Without another word, Daniel turned his back on Isaac and walked away.

"Daniel."

Daniel didn't look back or stop moving. He couldn't. Isaac was sorry. Fuck. He should be. No one could love him. Only a fucking idiot would fall in love with him. Tonight felt a lot like the night he wouldn't be able to do this any longer.

10

When Daniel first moved to New York, he would stand in the living room of his high-rise apartment and stare at the skyline. Back then, he'd thought there was no place more beautiful. New York City at night was like a lit-up Christmas tree. Now, with a bottle of Jack in one hand and a fifth of Crown inside him, Daniel wanted the Key Largo night sky back. Not just any night, though. He craved the one where Isaac had held him and done his damnedest to convince Daniel there was no place better.

Here Daniel was—thoroughly convinced and broken. He turned the bottle up. Fire licked at his throat. No doubt, in about five hours, Daniel would be hugging the toilet. That was okay. Rock bottom and puking up his guts is where Daniel deserved to be.

Isaac had fought tonight and won. Daniel had been there, hanging on every second. No one had screamed louder when the official raised Isaac's arm. The guy sitting behind Daniel had booed. The temptation to break something had been real. Isaac worked harder than any man alive. He sacrificed more than any other competitor. The crowd should've chanted Isaac's name. Daniel wished like hell he was currently crying Isaac's name.

After finding his phone, Daniel pulled up Isaac's many unanswered texts. There were apologies and angry rants as well as everything in between. The ache in his chest increased. Each time Daniel thought he couldn't hurt worse, he found a new level of pain. He'd walked away. Why the fuck had he done that? Why couldn't he think of a way to make it right?

After closing his messages, Daniel opened the notebook on his phone. He had a column due. For a few days now, he'd debated his words. Tonight's fight solidified his decision. He would make Isaac a star. It was the least he could do.

ISAAC WORKED at straightening Aden's office, finding spots for all the samples of protein powder that showed up almost on a daily basis. It was the last thing he needed to get done before he could leave for the night. Isaac had fallen into a depression he couldn't shake since Daniel walked away. Even though he recognized he wasn't really speaking to anyone, Isaac couldn't seem to stop. There was nothing to say. His life was empty. He showed up at scheduled matches, fought, and won. Isaac was at the gym almost daily, either working out or working his shift. Life went on without Daniel. A million times, Isaac had told himself they were temporary. He didn't know why his heart hadn't listened. Now he was getting what he deserved. He'd expected too much. Pushed too hard.

Unfortunately, Isaac couldn't seem to stop texting

Daniel. He always regretted it the moment he hit send. That didn't stop him from trying again hours later. Daniel's nonresponse hadn't stopped him either. He'd never considered himself needy or desperate. It seemed he simply hadn't met the right person before now.

Isaac could feel Remy's stare, boring a hole in the top of his head. He'd been working on paperwork at Aden's desk the whole time Isaac had been cleaning, but Isaac was certain the man hadn't done anything other than stare at him. Remy was an amazing person and a good friend. Still, Isaac couldn't drum up a single word for the man. No doubt, Remy knew something was wrong. There was no way people hadn't noticed Daniel's visits had stopped. Isaac couldn't force his lips to shape the words, admitting they were over. So he didn't speak at all. It was depressing, but as long as he didn't say the words, he could pretend they weren't true.

"Will we ever get to meet your daughter?" Remy said, finally breaking the silence.

His question shocked Isaac enough to turn him stupid. "What?"

Remy shrugged, looking uncomfortable, which was something Isaac never expected to see. "We trained together under Drew for a couple of years, and now you're living in our gym and training with my husband. I'm just a little surprised you still haven't introduced us to your daughter."

"She lives in California," Isaac said, hoping to hold up his end of the conversation while his brain scrambled to catch up.

"Yeah. Daniel's article said she goes to UCLA, but still. We've known each other for years. I would've thought I rated some sort of introduction. At least, over the holidays or something."

Isaac couldn't understand why his lips were numb. "Um, she'll be here for a couple of weeks at Christmas. Otherwise, she's only been here once—for two days while you were in New Orleans. I'm sorry, did you say something about an article?"

Remy smiled. "Yay. Two weeks with the daughter, and yeah. I thought you knew. Have you not seen Daniel's latest article?"

There it was again. Daniel's article. That was definitely what Remy had said twice now. Isaac wasn't hearing things. Shifting from foot to foot, Isaac fought to keep his feelings hidden. He'd been doing his damnedest not to think of Daniel. After another deep breath, Isaac risked speaking again. "Since I opened this morning, I haven't had time to check it out. I'll have to do that." Isaac gave himself a mental pat on the back. God only knew how he'd managed those words without his inner fury making him growl each syllable. He had to get out of here. "I hate to run out on you, but I have plans." He hoped they didn't involve killing Daniel. Isaac very much feared they did.

"Of course," Remy said, waving him away. "I'll see you tomorrow."

Isaac nodded and walked away. His feet carried him past at least three people who tried stopping him. He dipped his chin at each one, hoping they'd understand for once he didn't have time. Isaac didn't make it upstairs. The instant he turned the corner and was out of sight, Isaac pulled his phone out and found Daniel's latest article. Isaac's feet slowed before coming to a complete stop. He didn't know how much time passed as he stood, blinking down at the title of Daniel's column.

"The Secret Life of an Up-and-Coming Boxer."

He didn't need to read it. Whatever the article said was

an invasion of his privacy. A betrayal. Without a thought or plan, Isaac dialed Daniel's number. To his surprise, Daniel answered. "Hello?"

"You motherfucking bastard," Isaac said before he knew he would. "You wrote an article about my *daughter*." If he'd ever been more enraged in his life, Isaac couldn't recall it.

"I did you a favor," Daniel said, sounding calm. "When you fight Jericho, people will chant your name. Everyone loves a nice guy."

"Fuck. You. You know I don't give a shit if people chant my name. If you don't know that, fuck you twice. How dare you do this to me? Trina has never had a normal life. Now she never fucking will."

Daniel sighed. It sounded loud through the line. "I told you nothing is really off the record with me."

Isaac didn't respond. He couldn't. His throat and eyes burned. This was the man who'd stolen his heart. Isaac had thought Daniel had already done all the damage he could do to his heart. He'd been wrong. So very fucking wrong. Isaac swallowed, trying his damnedest to get words to push past his tight throat. "Is this my punishment for telling you that I love you?"

Daniel cleared his throat. When he spoke, his voice still didn't give a hint of his emotions. "This is all I can give you, Isaac. It's all I have to offer. Maybe it's not what you wanted when you said those words, but this is it. You might hate it, but that article will bend public opinion."

Isaac hurt. All the pain he'd been swallowing down since Daniel walked away was rising to choke him now. "I don't give a damn about public perception, Daniel. Even if your article hadn't exploited my daughter, I wouldn't have wanted it. I didn't want you for what you could do for me. I fell in love with you because no one else has ever made me feel the way you do. This fucking article," Isaac paused and drew a deep breath, trying to calm himself. "I would rather you'd told me you'll never love me back than do this to me, but whatever makes you feel better about yourself." He hung up before he could bare anymore of his soul to the man who'd stolen his heart and then destroyed him.

WHEN THE PHONE went dead in his hand, Daniel chucked it as hard as he could against the opposite wall. His shoulders heaved like he'd been running for miles. He didn't know what Isaac fucking wanted from him. When it came time for Isaac to fight Jericho, everyone would choose to cheer for a man who adopted a cancer patient over a fake ass any day. Isaac should've begged for him to write that piece.

The cold glass of his living room window did nothing to cool his temper when he pressed his forehead against the pane. The whole city looked dirty and gray. Before meeting Isaac, Daniel hadn't been home in at least six months. Since they'd been dating, he'd come more often, searching for himself—or the man he used to be, at least. Daniel thought —if he found that man—he could go back to being an emotionless robot. Once he'd let one emotion in, he'd stopped watching the gate, and they'd all flooded in. For someone like him, that was a disastrous thing.

Daniel loved Isaac. That was what he should've said when Isaac told Daniel he loved him on the beach. Instead, he'd reverted to being the basket case he'd been years ago, before his career had given him focus. Daniel sucked in a deep breath, filling his lungs and trying to calm his mind. He blew it back out, fogging up the window. With the tip of his finger, he drew faces in the fog. He kept his mind blank, concentrating on the ridiculous task as he purposely fogged up more of the window to make more faces. As Daniel drew a heart and added Isaac's name, Aden's office came to mind. All the colorful rainbows, hearts, and I love yous Remy had drawn. Both men let it ride, uncaring of who saw their insane love for each other. Aden was a grumpy bastard and Remy was the glitter queen. They shouldn't fit, but they did. Could Isaac and he be the same? Isaac was the kind-hearted hero and Daniel was the black-souled troll in designer shoes. They shouldn't fit, but they did. Daniel had ruined it by not being honest.

Turning away from the window, Daniel searched the room with his gaze. He spotted his phone sticking out from underneath the sofa where it had slid after bouncing off the wall. After retrieving it, he brushed off the face. This was the reason he'd sprung for an indestructible case. His temper ensured he'd throw his phone often. He'd needed something to withstand him.

Daniel opened his notebook app and got started. If Isaac felt one well-placed article had destroyed them, then Daniel would do one more, and ruin himself. If Isaac never spoke to him again, at least they'd be even. Hope swelled in Daniel's chest as he typed. Maybe, though. Just maybe, Isaac would understand and give Daniel another shot. He'd never been good at apologizing, but he did have words and a voice.

11

*D*espite the massive anger sitting on Isaac's throat and choking the life from him, every second without Daniel ticked by, feeling longer than the last. All he had was his work and training. His fight with Jericho was three weeks away. Most likely, he'd get his ass handed to him right before Christmas and days before getting to see Trina again. The sure knowledge he'd lose didn't stop Isaac from practicing and sparring every free second. Aden stayed later with him each night. Sometimes Remy stayed too. Other times, they were alone. Either way, Isaac felt guilty as hell for cutting into their time together. He wondered now why this had been so important to him. The closer the fight came to reality, the more Isaac wondered if it was worth it. Maybe he should've stayed in Vegas. At least he had family there. He was closer to Trina there. Here, he had nothing and what he did have didn't matter for shit.

Remy crossed the room. Isaac watched it happening with all the detachment he could muster. Today was another day of him going through the motions. He didn't want to chat.

"Have you read Daniel's latest article yet?"

Isaac turned his back on Remy at the question. He wished the man would let it drop. "I've been busy."

"You're not too busy for this," Remy said, snagging his arm and dragging him toward the office.

Isaac tried getting away. "I need to wipe down the machines."

"I'm your goddamn boss," Remy said without slowing. "If anyone knows what you need to be doing, it's me, and I say you should be coming with me."

Since Isaac couldn't argue that logic, he let Remy drag him inside the office and push him down into a chair. He turned away to get something from Aden's desk, and Isaac eyed the door. There was a real chance he could make it to the front door before Remy caught him.

"Don't fucking move," Remy barked as if he had eyes in the back of his head. After finding what he'd been searching for, Remy moved to stand over Isaac. He handed him an iPad. Daniel's article was already pulled up. Isaac stared at the man's picture, nestled at the top corner of the words filling the screen. The ache in his chest was crippling. It wasn't often he let himself care about anyone. He loved Daniel. It wouldn't die no matter how much the man's betrayal hurt. When Isaac didn't take the tablet, Remy shook it at him. "Read the piece," he said in a tone that let Isaac know he wouldn't be avoiding this.

With no other choice left to him, Isaac accepted the tablet, and read.

My Secret Life

"Over the years, I've written thousands of articles. Not once have I been the subject of one. My freshman year of college, before I was anywhere near earning my degree in journalism, I met William Pettifore while interning for the Daily Sports

Report. *He saw something in me and took a chance. The rest was history. For fifteen years, I've worked for this paper. Back then, we actually were a paper. People subscribed and followed every word. Now, everything is online and ads keep us in business, but the readers—they're my passion."*

It was odd. So far, the article Daniel had written hadn't said anything special, but Isaac could feel how much Daniel meant his words. He loved his job. Isaac couldn't stop reading about it.

"For years, I've traveled the country, attending every event imaginable. I've met super stars at the height of their careers—done interviews with athletes at their lowest. When Gunnar Samson won the Heavyweight title belt, I was the first interview he gave. When Jai Kelley became the scandal of the hockey season after his sex tapes were leaked to the press, I had the exclusive. I've been blessed to not have to spend a second of my time sitting still, alone with my thoughts. No one would want a moment with my mind."

Isaac wasn't sure he blinked as he read. He could hear Daniel's voice saying each word, but Isaac still couldn't picture Daniel having a single problem.

"You see, I've spent years uncovering secrets and sharing them with the world without once shining a light on my own. That ends today. Here's the story about my life that no one knows. I'm a manic depressive."

Isaac stared at the words, reading them several times without absorbing them. They didn't fit the image he had of Daniel. Daniel had never struck him as unhappy. He had to know.

"For me, it's been easy to embrace the manic side. As long as I keep moving, the depressive side stays at bay—for the most part. Until recently, this secret wasn't important to anyone other than me. It didn't matter if I fell into black moods, shutting out anyone

who cares about me, because I pushed those people away years ago. No one cared if I disappeared and drank myself into oblivion. That is, until recently. A year and a half ago, I met the most amazing Upstart. For professional purposes, I've kept a close eye on his career. It's been my heart that's kept me enthralled by the rest of him."

Each breath Isaac took came harder than the last. Disbelief owned him.

"Recently, I used my position with this paper to betray his trust. I printed a story he'd told me in confidence. At the time, I didn't see my story for what it was—self-destruction. In the back of my mind, without realizing it, I'd somewhere along line convinced myself he'd be better off without me in his life. Sadly, for people like me, this isn't uncommon behavior. If he reads this, I'm sorry for hurting you. I was wrong. You deserved better. My love isn't worth much, but you have it. For everyone else who's reading this and wondering what this has to do with sports, all I have to say is—everything. Every day, athletes suffer from life-altering head injuries..."

Isaac didn't see the rest of the article. A haze coated his vision. It was an apology he never expected to see. In the most public way possible. Daniel hadn't named him, but it wouldn't be hard for people to figure out who the article was about. They'd been seen together several times by countless people. So, Daniel could tell the world, but not him. That was fine.

He handed the tablet back to Remy and stood. "I've got equipment to wipe down." Remy's shoulders fell. Isaac couldn't let the man's dejection get under his skin. He'd told Daniel he loved him. The man had walked away. All the articles in the world couldn't fix things if Daniel kept hiding behind his keyboard. They wouldn't make up for all the unanswered texts and calls. One fucking truth-baring article didn't make up for Daniel breaking his heart.

Isaac headed for the back, intent on grabbing some paper towels. Remy was hot on his heels. "You're not alone, Isaac."

Aden stepped into his path, leaving him no choice but to stop running. Isaac snapped. "Look. I don't want to talk about it."

Aden held up a pair of boxing gloves. His expression remained blank. "Let's get you into these gloves. You have a lot of work to do before your fight."

Without a word, Isaac dipped his chin in a sharp nod. Hitting something sounded great.

THE DAYS LEADING up to his fight with Jericho crept by. They should've flown. Isaac hadn't gotten to sit still for even a moment. He'd worked his ass off in the ring and to avoid reporters. Everyone had questions. Isaac still didn't want to talk to anyone about anything. It was as if Daniel had walked away, taking Isaac's voice with him. Now that he was here, standing in the center of a Vegas boxing ring, listening to the rules being read and tuning out the crowd, Isaac realized he had a lot to say. There were millions of unspoken words inside his head. All of them were screaming Daniel's name. Unadulterated fury filled Isaac. He fucking loved Daniel. It was all Daniel's fault too. He'd been the one who gave Isaac everything and then expected Isaac not to feel. Fuck that. Isaac wasn't a robot. If Daniel hadn't wanted Isaac to feel anything, the man should've bought a goddamn blowup doll, because now he had Isaac's heart. It didn't matter if he didn't want it.

The bell rang. Isaac bounced forward and landed a solid blow to the side of Jericho's head. The crowd roared. Jericho's expression was priceless. It was obvious he hadn't expected Isaac to be much of a challenge or to come out swinging. In truth, Isaac wasn't even thinking. There'd been no style to the move. He was just so goddamn angry. Isaac didn't know where to go with it. He'd held his tongue. Kept himself in check. He'd submitted and let Daniel control him. All he'd wanted was one fucking thing from the man— his heart. Daniel couldn't even give him that. The fucker. Isaac swung again with enough force Jericho couldn't block him. This time, Isaac's glove connected with Jericho's left eye.

Isaac wasn't avoiding hits. Jericho had gotten a couple in as well. They weren't fazing Isaac. He wasn't feeling a thing past the rage in his chest. It didn't matter his anger wasn't directed at Jericho. The man was simply in his way when Isaac finally broke. Another bell rang, signaling the end of the round. Isaac went to his corner. Aden was working as his cornerman. He spoke. Isaac didn't hear any of it. His gaze remained locked on Jericho. It was a threat. Life had been kicking Isaac his whole goddamn life. Now this man stood between Isaac and seeing Daniel again. He would win this fight. Daniel would interview him. The man would fucking love him if it was the last thing Isaac did.

DANIEL STARED at his TV in disbelief. Isaac's fury rolled off him in waves for anyone to see. The bell rang, starting the second round. Isaac headed for Jericho. Daniel came to his feet. He didn't know if Isaac's intent was obvious to everyone or if Daniel knew the man better than anyone else. Either way, Daniel held his breath while refusing to blink. He wasn't disappointed. There was zero style in Isaac's next move. He crossed the ring, eating up the space between Jericho and him. In a single swing, he knocked the man out cold. Even once it was over, Daniel couldn't blink. Jericho didn't move. The count was read even though it was pointless. They'd be carrying Jericho from the ring.

Isaac's arm was raised in victory. Daniel sat and turned the TV off. His mind wouldn't slow. That hadn't been Isaac. Maybe it was him in body, but that was all. No one had pushed Isaac like Daniel had, and he'd never seen that angry version of Isaac. Was that his fault? Was this what he'd done to the man he loved? Daniel wasn't surprised he'd ruined someone, but then again, he was. He'd stupidly believed Isaac couldn't be damaged. Isaac was better than everyone else in every way.

Daniel's cellphone rang. He answered without thought. "Hello?"

"When can I expect that exclusive on my desk?"

Daniel stared at the now blank TV screen, searching his memories. It wasn't like him to forget something that important. "What exclusive?"

"That Isaac Jones guy who just beat Jericho Williams," Phil explained. "He just told Chris Knight with The Boxing Network that he promised the exclusive to you. Good job. When can I expect it? It needs to go live before everything he has to say is old news."

"I just need to book a flight," Daniel said, hoping he didn't sound as dead inside as he felt. He'd bared the secret he'd sworn to never reveal, and he'd done it in front of the whole damn world—for Isaac. It had been for nothing. The man never even called. Now Isaac was giving Daniel the exclusive. How magnanimous. Daniel barely stopped himself from rolling his eyes at his own sarcasm.

"Get whatever they have ASAP. I've already spoken to his trainer. Aden gave me the man's hotel room number in Vegas. I'll text you the details. And, Daniel, I want that article by tomorrow night."

After releasing a slow breath, hoping to temper his reaction, Daniel managed to sound halfway normal. "Yes, sir. I'm on it."

"Good," Phil said before hanging up without saying goodbye. Daniel was used to it.

He tried damn hard to clear his mind as he searched flight times on his phone. There was one he could make before the end of the night. Since it took six hours to get from New York to Vegas, Daniel could sleep on the plane and be with Isaac by the morning. Daniel shook his head. Being with Isaac wasn't what this was about. This was just an interview. It had to be about nothing more than doing his job. Anything else might kill him.

12

*D*aniel took the elevator to the eighth floor and then the stairs to the twelfth. Since everyone had obviously heard Isaac promise him the exclusive, Daniel couldn't be too careful. He didn't want any crazies following him up to Isaac's room. At six a.m., it was possible Isaac was still sleeping. Hell, he might not even be in his room yet. There was a very real probability Isaac had found another man to spend the night celebrating with. Daniel couldn't breathe at the thought. He'd known Isaac was special from the moment they met. Now the world would know it. Isaac could have his pick without the fame, but he had the fame now.

At Isaac's door, Daniel wiped his hands on his pants. He'd changed his clothes and brushed his teeth in the airport bathroom. Since he was used to living his life on the go, it was nowhere near the first time, but this time, he felt woefully unprepared for this meeting.

Daniel's knuckles barely skimmed the door before it opened. Amber eyes stared out at him. His expression gave nothing away. There was a bruise on his jaw. Daniel couldn't stop looking at Isaac. Before that moment, he hadn't realized eyes could miss someone. He knew it now. His eyes craved the sight of Isaac and didn't want to miss soaking up every detail.

"Hey."

At Isaac's greeting, Daniel's gaze slid to the man's mouth. "Hey."

Isaac took a step back. "Come in."

Daniel's grip tightened on his phone as he stepped inside the room. Once he crossed the threshold enough for Isaac to close the door, Daniel froze. Even though Isaac was in a suite, Daniel could still see the bed through the open doorway. It was still made. His empty stomach churned.

Isaac motioned toward the table. "Please, sit."

Despite his inability to stop looking at Isaac, the moment his ass hit the chair, Daniel argued against being there. "I'm here because I'm paid to be."

Isaac nodded as he sat across from Daniel. "Understood. Ask your questions."

"Are you seeing anyone?" The question slipped out, shocking Daniel. He hadn't meant to ask. This interview wasn't about them. His boss had demanded it of him. Isaac had beat Jericho. That was huge. This was Isaac's moment. What the fuck was wrong with him?

Isaac's expression never changed. He nodded. "I am." Daniel's insides twisted and burned like acid. If he'd stuck to his usual script—gotten his interview and gotten out—he wouldn't have to know this. His ignorance could've been his bliss.

He did his damnedest to keep his face blank. "I apologize. Let's stick to your career."

"No. It's okay," Isaac assured him with a small smile. "I don't mind talking about him. He took me to lunch a year and a half ago. I thought he'd decided he didn't like me, because he didn't call afterward."

Daniel's throat tightened. He could barely speak. "I guess you were wrong." It was the best he could come up with under the circumstances.

Isaac pulled a face. "That's what I thought too, but he didn't show up for my fight last night. I thought I meant more to him than that."

"He sounds like an idiot," Daniel said, trying not to let hope destroy him. His heart didn't want to be beat into submission.

Isaac's amber gaze never wavered from Daniel's face. "He can be sometimes. But I love him," Isaac added, sounding so damn sure.

"Why? He doesn't sound very lovable."

Isaac's mouth lifted in one corner. "That's only because you've never seen the way he looks at me."

Daniel swallowed past the lump that kept getting larger. He couldn't play along with this any longer. He had real issues. "The day you found me drunk in my hotel room, that wasn't even a bad day. It had been just a slightly off day."

"Maybe, but it was still a great night," Isaac said with a knowing smile, as if he remembered every detail.

Even though Daniel couldn't argue with Isaac's point, he still found a way to keep trying. "That's another thing. Hyper sexuality is a side effect of my condition. I can't stop myself in those moments from taking what I want from you."

Isaac cocked his head to one side and studied Daniel's face. "Are you listing things you think I won't like? I can't tell. Just because I didn't know about the depression thing doesn't mean that I don't know you."

He didn't know how to make Isaac understand something he couldn't understand. "I can't explain what's it's like inside my head, Isaac. It can get dark, and I can't control it. When you said you loved me, I was terrified of myself in that moment. I don't want to make the inside of your head as ugly as mine." It didn't matter if his reasoning didn't make sense to Isaac. It was Daniel's truth. The logical part of his brain said he wasn't contagious. Logic had nothing to do with this. He couldn't outsmart the thoughts that sneaked in, whispering he was a disease.

"So take charge of what you can," Isaac whispered, luring him in. "Control me."

Daniel shook his head and stood. "You don't want this. I have to go."

"What about our interview?" Isaac asked, following him to the door.

"I'll make something up."

The air squeezed from Daniel's lungs as Isaac's arms tightened around him, dragging him back against a hard chest. His lips touched Daniel's ear. Daniel couldn't move. He was trapped by more than Isaac's strength. His body had shut down, losing the ability to move from Isaac's hold.

"I love you," Isaac said against the shell of Daniel's ear. Daniel's throat threatened to swell closed at the words. "I love you," Isaac repeated. "You don't have to say it back. Hell, you don't have to feel it, but you won't ignore me," Isaac said, sounding like it was more of a threat than a promise. "You can control me in our bed. I want it. Need it. But you will not walk away from me again. I won't hand you all the power just to watch you turn into a pussy when things get too real." His grip tightened on Daniel's jaw, holding him in place. "I love you."

Daniel swallowed. His eyes fell closed.

"You can make me come and get down on my knees. If

you want me tied down, I'm there. But you cannot make me stop loving you. If you were ever going to fight for anyone, fight for me," Isaac begged, making Daniel's eyes burn. "You don't want to test me. Don't make me chase you."

Daniel didn't realize he was stroking Isaac's arm around his waist until the man's hold tightened.

"I bought a house." The admission slipped from Daniel with no real plan. Once it was out there, Daniel couldn't stop. "For us," Daniel added. "Two miles from the gym and three doors down from Aden." The more he admitted, the stronger Daniel's voice got. "I bought it a month ago. Three days before you told me you love me."

Isaac's hold didn't slacken. "Why?"

Daniel blew out a steady breath. "Because I love you and I want to be with you. Because I won't stop coming back for more and I want to give you everything."

A soft kiss landed beneath Daniel's ear. His heart turned over in his chest at the sensation. The grip on his jaw transformed into a loving caress. "Daniel."

The sweet way Isaac whispered his name had Daniel weak at the knees.

"This is where you belong. Right here with me," Isaac punctuated his words by burying his hand beneath Daniel's shirt, going skin on skin. "I'm not afraid of your worst days, but I'm scared as fuck of never holding you again."

The terror was in Isaac's voice. Daniel heard it in every word. No one had ever been so raw—exposed their heart to him the way Daniel did. "Isaac." Even Daniel heard the desperation in his one word. "I don't want to hurt you."

"Then don't," Isaac said as if it was the simplest thing in the world. He turned Daniel in his arms. He cupped Daniel's face, leaving him no other choice than to hold his gaze. "I love you," Isaac said, sounding so sure Daniel couldn't deny it. "Don't leave me again."

"I love you too," Daniel said, because it was what he should've said over a month ago. He'd lost his chance then. Daniel wouldn't ruin it this time too. Isaac's eyes fell closed, as if he'd been waiting for those words for a lifetime. Daniel kissed him. It was out of his control. Those were his lips. Isaac belonged to him.

With no clue as to how it happened, Daniel found his back against the wall and Isaac's hand kneading his cock through his pants. "Don't leave again," Isaac repeated through their kisses. "You're the one for me. I'd find you."

Daniel clung to Isaac's shoulders, holding on for dear life while trying to get as close as possible while riding the man's palm. "I bought you a house. I can't leave."

To his surprise, Isaac laughed against his lips. "Goddamn you, Daniel. This is all your fault."

Daniel pulled away and met Isaac's gaze. "Probably, but you'll have to be more specific."

Isaac took Daniel's hand and led it to the hard cock hidden behind Isaac's zipper. "Now I'll be miserable all day, walking around like this."

"Not if I can help it," Daniel said with all the desire he felt.

A rueful smile pulled at Isaac's lips. "My mom is supposed to be here any minute. She's taking us to breakfast."

Daniel blinked. His mind blank. "Us? What?"

Isaac's smile grew. "Well, me, but now you're here. So we're both going."

"We are?" Daniel's desire fled under the weight of his panic.

A knock sounded beside his head. Isaac couldn't have

looked smugger. Before Daniel could make a run for it, Isaac dipped his head and stole another kiss. While he reeled from the power of the man's touch, Isaac answered the door. A mocha-skinned woman with Isaac's beautiful smile stepped inside. Her outfit looked familiar. The memory hit Daniel. Isaac had said she was a black jack dealer at one of the casinos. She must be working.

She eyed him. If she was confused over Daniel's presence, she didn't show it. "You must be Daniel," she said, holding her hand out for him to shake. He accepted. She didn't release it right away. "Isaac said he wasn't sure if you'd make it. I'm glad you did."

Even to him, Daniel's smile felt strained. "It's nice to meet you, Mrs. Jones."

"Please call me Pam."

"Pam," he repeated while still trying to gather his thoughts.

"You must be jetlagged," she said, supplying him with an excuse.

He nodded. "Yes, ma'am. My flight landed an hour ago. I slept on the plane, but I'm still adjusting to the time change."

She moved so fast he almost took a step back and ruined the moment. Pam hugged him. "I'm just so thrilled to finally meet you," she said, explaining the abrupt gesture. "Isaac has been telling me about you for months, but we keep missing each other. I'm sure your job keeps you busy, but here you are. Did you really fly all night to be here?"

Daniel's gaze flickered between Isaac and her. He'd never expected Isaac had been talking to his family about him. "I did."

"That's so sweet." Her gushing words had him blushing.

"We have a surprise for you," Isaac said, stealing his mom's focus.

Daniel's eyebrows rose. He was as clueless as Pam, especially since he knew next to nothing about her and hadn't been expecting to meet her today.

She danced in place. "What? I love surprises."

Isaac moved to Daniel's side, took his hand, and pulled him closer. "Well, really it was my surprise too. Daniel bought us a house in Key Largo. We're moving in together." As Pam squealed and hugged them, Daniel smiled while trying to decide if he would kill Isaac later or fuck him senseless.

"I never expected my baby would settle down. You're such a miracle maker. I can't believe this is happening."

That made two of them.

13

"*D*idn't I just help you move?"

Isaac winked at Remy. "Yes, and I love you for it."

Daniel slapped his ass. "Don't wink at other men."

"But it's okay for him to tell my husband he loves him? That's fucked up," Aden bitched as he walked by, carrying a huge box.

Daniel shrugged. "Everyone loves your husband. You'll just have to suck it up."

Isaac unscrewed the cap on his drink and turned the drink up.

Remy turned away from the box he was unpacking. "When are the two of you getting married?"

To Isaac's surprise, as he choked on his drink, Daniel laughed. "I'm waiting to spring it on Isaac when his parents are around and we haven't had much time to discuss things."

"Oh, okay," Remy said, as if that was the normal way of doing things. "Do you at least have a ring?"

"You gotta have a ring, man," Aden said, strolling through with another box but somehow still keeping up with conversation. "You need a kickass ring if you want the kickass guy."

"Of course I have a ring," Daniel said, causing Isaac to whip around in his direction. "I wouldn't buy a man a house unless I'd also bought a ring. This isn't a playhouse."

Remy waved off Daniel's claim. "There's no reason it can't be both. I like to play in my house."

Isaac couldn't stop looking around at everyone, wondering if they'd lost their minds. It had been just over a month since Daniel had dropped the bomb on his mom. They'd chosen to spend the holidays with Isaac's parents and then move after the first. The man had run from Isaac when he'd told him he loved him. Now Daniel was chitchatting with their friends about marriage without a hint of fear, and as if it was a done deal.

Isaac grabbed his bottle of water and headed for the bedroom. "I think I'll get started on the bedroom and leave the three of you alone to plan my wedding."

Remy looked up from the box he was buried in and flashed Isaac a sweet smile. "Okay. I love planning out pretty things."

They were all so damn serious. Isaac didn't know what to think. Once he was all alone in the bedroom, he set his water on the dresser and stood in the center of the room. They'd bought a new bed. It was theirs—Daniel and his. This was where'd they sleep side by side for the rest of their lives, as a married couple at some point, apparently. He wasn't freaking out. At least, he didn't think he was. Daniel's arms wrapped around his waist. His lips brushed Isaac's neck. "Okay. What's wrong?"

Isaac didn't even consider dodging. "First I scare you and now you have a ring?"

"You don't scare me. I scare me, but you trust me, so I don't intend to let you down. This is forever, Isaac. Are you denying it?"

"No."

"Okay, then," Daniel said, dropping his hand and cupping Isaac's cock. "Why are you arguing?"

"I'm not." He covered Daniel's hand, stopping him from getting Isaac any harder than he was already working on being. "Aden and Remy are here."

"Actually, Aden just remembered he left the coffee pot on at their house. He needed Remy to go with him to check."

"Smooth," Isaac said with a laugh. The pair was a mess. They couldn't keep their hands off each other. Isaac got it.

He felt Daniel nod against his shoulder. "I thought so. Personally, I think we should take notes. I foresee lots of sneaking away to be alone in our future."

"We're alone right now," Isaac reminded him.

Daniel popped the button on Isaac's shorts and slipped his hand inside. "I foresee a lot of other things in our future as well."

"Such as?" Isaac asked, leaning his head back against Daniel's shoulder and enjoying the sensation of Daniel handling his cock.

"Agree to marry me and I'll give you a list."

"There was never any chance I'd say no. Where's my list?"

"Strip and I'll show you the future," Daniel said, moving to occupy the chair, obviously intent on watching the show.

Isaac pulled his shirt over his head and tossed it aside. He didn't need Daniel to show him the future. He'd seen it the moment Daniel had invited him back to his room almost two years ago. They were perfect when they were together, and Isaac would never let them be apart.

THE END

Keep an eye out for the next book in the series, Gatekeeper.

ABOUT THE AUTHOR

Charity Parkerson is an award winning and multi-published author with several companies. Born with no filter from her brain to her mouth, she decided to take this odd quirk and insert it in her characters.

*2015 Readers' Favorite Award Winner
  *Winner of 2, 2014 Readers' Favorite Awards
  *2015 Passionate Plume Award Finalist
  *2013 Readers' Favorite Award Winner
  *2013 Reviewers' Choice Award Winner
  *2012 ARRA Finalist for Favorite Paranormal Romance
  *Five-time winner of The Mistress of the Darkpath

Connect with her online:

--Join my street team: facebook.com/TeamCharityParkerson
  --Sign up for her newsletter: http://bit.ly/CharityNews
  --Website: charityparkerson.com
  --Facebook: facebook.com/authorCharityParkerson
  facebook.com/TheMenofSin
  --Twitter: twitter.com/CharityParkerso

www.charityparkerson.com